BROKEN ANGEL

THE UMAROVA CRIME FAMILY
SERIES
BOOK 1

IVY BLACK
AND
ELIZABETH KNOX

ISBN: 9798375868110
Copyright © 2023. All rights reserved.

It is not legal to reproduce, duplicate, or transmit any part of this document in either electronic means or in printed format. Recording of this publication is strictly prohibited and any storage of this document is not allowed unless with written permission from the publisher except for the use of brief quotations in a book review.

This is a work of fiction. Any resemblance to actual persons, living or dead, or actual events is purely coincidental.

Your Exclusive Access

From the bottom of our hearts, thank you so much for your support.

To show our appreciation, we've created an exclusive VIP newsletter just for you. When you join, you'll immediately receive a free prequel you won't find anywhere else!

You will also receive bonus chapters, notifications of future releases, future discounts, and many more surprises!

Download the prequel, receive future discounts and other bonuses by visiting: https://BookHip.com/MXSLKNV

See you on the inside,
Ivy Black and Elizabeth Knox

Prologue

Ruslan

Present Day

The distinctive creaking of metal is the only familiar noise I hear these days. The wind gusts crash hard against the walls of the metal fishing shack. I try to hold back my frustrated grunt. It sounds like an old whistle that never seems to stop, and it aggravates me. I don't know how long I've been here. I'm going to assume it's been a couple of days, but I've been drugged. For all I know, it could be longer.

Truthfully, I don't remember much about my travels. When I was being lugged into this building or rather a shack, I do remember certain imagery. I recall what looked to be a rusty fishing shed with buoys and nets hanging on the outside. I recall the scent of salty water and hearing birds. Then everything went black again.

After that, I woke up strapped to a chair. My binds aren't loose in the least bit, and the chair they've strapped me to isn't even metal. It's as old and rickety as this shack is, and I know I'll have an advantage at some point. I could move my body back and forth, ultimately crushing the wood behind me and freeing myself, but I want answers. I want to know why Artos betrayed me. And right now, I don't have that answer, and I'm unsure when I will.

This isn't the first time I've ever been held captive, and I'm certain it won't be the last. Since my time here, I've only seen one person come in and out of the shack. At first, it was like my vision was blurred. I could see a figure, but I couldn't make out any details. When the man spoke, it was very gravelly, and it sounded like he could've very well smoked cigarettes for most of his life.

I notice a clear bag hanging above me, which funnels directly into my right arm. There's a plethora of solutions they could be filling me up with. I'd like to hope it's simply saline to keep me hydrated and alive, but it could be poison for all I know. If it's the latter, it could explain why my vision is still fuzzy. Regardless, when I get out of here, someone's going to have hell to pay.

I think back to the circumstances that led me here, and even as my memories plague my mind, I have a hard time understanding why Artos betrayed me.

"The Armenians have been here, and I've heard they're intimidating you to do business with them, or rather let them run their business from your gas station?"

The man nods, but then he speaks in a stuttered manner. "Yes, s-sir. I h-haven't said they c-could do anything. They're very... very determined to get m-me to do things I don't w-want to do." the more this man speaks, the more I don't feel bad for him.

I begin to walk the aisles of the gas station and start pushing things over, knocking them off the shelves, and then I approach the lighter fluid. I grab a bottle, pop the top off, and pour the liquid all over the place. I put it on the shelves, the merchandise, anywhere I can possibly get a drop of this stuff on.

I take a lighter out of my pocket and flick it on, causing the shop owner's eyes to widen even further. "Look! I haven't done a-anything wrong! I am only a man who is trying to s-support his family," he pleads with me, but his pleas won't be enough.

"If you work with the Armenians, you will lose everything and have no way to feed your family. Do you understand me? No one who has loyalty to the Umarova family is permitted to do business with my enemies."

The shop owner nods and goes quiet, but he quickly speaks up. "What of the

Celtic who works for you? He doesn't have your best interests in mind. He works against you. Don't you know it?" I look into the man's eyes, and I know a liar when I see one. This man isn't lying and has everything to lose by telling me this.

Just then, the gas station door opens, and Artos comes walking in. "Boss, I figured you might want a familiar face to deal with this one."

The shop owner and I stare at each other for a moment, but I break the space between Artos and me. I grab the bastard by the back of the neck and slam him into one of the shelves. His body comes crashing against it, and the shelf hits the floor.

Artos rises and charges toward me. I notice him reaching into his pocket, but I'm trying to keep his body weight off mine. He comes at me full charge, and at the same time, he pushes on me with his left arm, and a prickling sensation shoots down my neck.

I begin to stumble forward, and my vision grows blurry. I hit the ground with a thud and attempt to move my hands, but as I stare at my hands, it looks like they're melting. I don't think they are, but my vision is deceiving me. I somehow manage to roll onto my back. The gas station owner is yelling at Artos and vice versa.

"You told me I wouldn't have to worry about a thing, and here he is! You lied to me! Why? Why lie to me when I do work for you!" the gas station owner screams.

Artos reaches for his gun and shoots the owner of the gas station point blank. His body falls to the ground, and blood begins to intermix with the lighter fluid. Artos comes to me, kneels down, and yanks me up by my hair. His smile is sinister as ever, and before I know it, everything is turning black.

A large gust of wind shakes the entire shack, and items from the outside fall and crash against the dock. The door squeaks every time the wind picks up and slows down, and then the door opens wider. For a moment, I think it's the wind, but as a dark shadow fills the doorframe, I realize it isn't the wind. It's the old man.

This time I can make out his face and see him almost as clear as day. Things are still a bit blurry, but not overly so. He has wrinkles in the center of his forehead, and his skin hangs a bit below his chin. Age spots riddle his skin, and he stares at me disgustingly. He runs a hand along his brittle white beard that hangs down to the center of his chest.

"Want to tell me what's bothering you, old man?" I ask, but my voice doesn't even sound like it's my own.

The man shuts the door behind him and latches it with a hook on the top and another on the bottom. As he moves, I realize even though he's older, he's quite stocky. "I must need to increase your dosage. You're too chatty," the man tells me in broken English with pauses between his words.

"I'm a man deserving of answers." It's the first time I've spoken to him, and with any luck, he'll give me some of what I'm looking for. Finding out the IV fluids coming into me have something to do with the dizziness I'm experiencing means I need to move quickly. I don't have the luxury of waiting until the old man leaves to get out of this mess. I need to act quickly, possibly while he's here. He might be broad-shouldered and appear like he could handle his own, though I'm confident I can take him on if given the opportunity.

The man shakes his head and scoffs. "You already have them. If only you'd just look." He begins to walk toward the bag, but I keep him talking. If I can distract him long enough, he might forget about shoving more of this shit in my body.

"Do I? Do I really have them?" I snap at the old man until he's staring directly at me in the eyes. Good. I have his attention. "One of my best men betrayed me out of the blue. A man whose hands my life has been laid in many times before. He could've killed me when he had the chance, but he didn't, so why does he betray me now? Hmm? Don't tell me the answer is right in front of me because it's bullshit."

"My, you are spirited. It's simple, really. You only have to look, Ruslan. It's all you have to do, and yet you don't even make an effort. You upset the order of things."

I upset the order of things? I replay the last few months in my head, and every bit of my work was done normally. I'm very particular about how I manage business dealings, but there's one thing that jumps out. I told off my stepfather in my family home. I told him exactly what I thought and didn't regret doing it.

My father was the head of the Umarova family. In the Chechen Republic, our name is law. Our family has been there since the start of the region, so we're well respected and feared. My father was murdered, and then everything changed. For a while, we weren't as feared as we should've been. As the eldest of my family, it would've been my right to lead, but I wasn't old enough.

My mother decided to remarry rather quickly out of fear for herself and her children being killed. It was just me, her, and my younger brother Lom at the time. Then she married my stepfather and had two more children later on. Marrying him kept her safe to some extent, but she named him a regent for the Umarova name, seeing as I was a child.

Now, I'm very much an adult, and my stepfather didn't want to let go of the reigns. When I confronted him, I told him he had no power since he wasn't an Umarova. I began doing things to take over my father's business, and I gather he didn't like it. But here's the thing: he isn't my father. He never had any right to lead, and he's been in his position for too long.

"My stepfather is a fraud. A vile pig. If you mean to stand there and lecture me, don't waste your breath," I snarl at the older man, who raises both of his brows. He stares at me for a moment and then laughs.

"You are a stupid, idiotic child. Do you not know the lengths he will go to keep what he believes is his? Do you even think about the lengths he's already gone to? Hmm?" As he finishes speaking, the door blows open, and the latches break off. The old man scrambles to find something to keep the door shut, and I know this is my opportunity.

I swing forward and then crash backward with all my body weight. The middle piece connecting my arms to the wood breaks, and my legs are unbound, so I rise to my feet. I yank my right hand as hard as I can, and it's just enough to slip my hand out. I'd been working on the ropes all day, hoping everything would go according to plan.

I rush up to the old man, and he swings around with a shocked expression on his face. He reaches over to the counter, where I can assume the owners of this shack filet fish, and grabs a knife. He waves it around in the air and walks toward me. I jump back as he tries to cut me across my abdomen and push him back. He stumbles but catches himself and charges at me. I move to the right, not noticing a bottle on the ground. I lose my footing and start to fall backward.

The old man stabs me right as I'm in mid-air. He pulls the knife out of me once I hit the ground and then stabs me again. "You're foolish to fight against me!" he screams in my face, and I refuse to go down without a fight. I reach up and grab the old man's eyes, pressing inward as hard as I can. The old man begins to scream, and then I feel a prick against my neck.

Out of nowhere, everything gets fuzzy. Floaters fill my vision, and I glance to the left where the stinging sensation's coming from. Sure enough, I spot a syringe hanging with the plunger fully depressed.

I then look down at my abdomen, and my blood is oozing out onto the floor around me. Fuck, what did I get myself into?

Is this how I'm going to die?

Chapter One

Amelia

The heavy rain from this summer storm crashes down on my windshield. I've just gotten home from work, but it's raining too hard for me to get out of the vehicle right now. I might just sit in here and wait for the storm to pass. There's a long way to walk on the path before I reach my apartment, and I'm not trying to get drenched.

Things don't feel right at all. To say I'm nervous would be a massive understatement. Ruslan, my sort-of boyfriend, has been AWOL for over four weeks. He left me a note saying he had to fly back home to handle some business, so I expected him to maybe be gone for a week, possibly two. Only, he never came back to Atlanta. The note said he'd be gone for a few days, and he left me money to make sure I was taken care of while he was away.

Ruslan is very well off and comes from money, but the two of us didn't meet under normal circumstances. I was a new hire at the notorious nightclub, Illusion. It's centered in the middle of Atlanta and is owned by the Steele family, who are like royalty around here. I'm pretty much convinced they own the entire city.

When I was first hired at Illusion, there was a robbery the same day. Someone came into the club and stole a large sum of money from the owner. Apparently, the security cameras cut off around the same time my interview happened, making me look like I was the guilty party.

Ruslan was sent to persuade me to give the money back. There's only one problem. How was I supposed to give back the money I didn't take in the first place? I had to convince Ruslan I was innocent, which took some convincing. He assumed I was lying, and I'm sure many people in the same position lie about it. The only difference is that I wasn't lying. After I convinced him I wasn't a bold-faced liar, he said he'd stick out his neck for me. I didn't understand what it meant, but Ruslan eventually told me he was taking sole responsibility for paying back my debt. There was a catch, though. I had to pay him back, doing whatever he wanted me to do.

I still had my job at Illusion on the weekends, but I also worked for Ruslan. But Ruslan's work wasn't like my work at Illusion. I wasn't some skimpy-dressed bottle service girl for Ruslan. No, it was kinky, provocative, and downright illegal. It was borderline prostitution in a way, but it somehow became less about paying Ruslan back and more about following my heart.

There was so much going on when all of this started. My life was a certified shitshow, hands down. I was in a loveless relationship with a piece of shit guy named Carter. I won't even call him a man because he wasn't one. He couldn't take any initiative, and he was nothing more than a scamming asshole. Deep in my gut, I think he was the person behind the money going missing at Illusion. Also, my identity was stolen over a year ago, and I've been dealing with hell from that. I wouldn't be surprised if Carter was behind it all. I'm only going to be able to get confirmation if I find actual proof, so until then, it's just my own speculation.

The rain finally starts to let up, so I sling my purse over my shoulder, take my keys out of the ignition, and make a run for it. I slam the car door too hard, but whatever. I guess it doesn't really matter. Even though I'm running, I still get pretty wet. It's no longer a torrential downpour, but the weather tends to change very fast around here.

I finally get under the safety of the porch, and I slide my keys around on the holder until I find the one for our apartment. I insert the key into the lock and turn the knob. It pops open freely, and I kick off my shoes as I enter. The one thing I hate about being a bottle girl is how I have to wear heels all the time. Some nights, my feet feel like they're literally killing me when I get home.

I hang my purse on the coat hook and walk further into my place. My cousin, Emily, just moved in with me about a month ago. She's going for her master's in commercial real estate at Georgia State University. If she moved in with me, she'd get a lower tuition rate, so it made sense for both of us. She'd help me save some money on rent, and she'd save thousands of dollars a year at the same time.

The heavy feeling in my chest is still there as my mind floats back to Ruslan. I said I was going to call his right-hand man, Danill, but I haven't done it yet. I don't know why I'm so afraid to call. Part of me thinks it's because Danill's going to tell me Ruslan's perfectly fine but isn't coming back.

As much as I want to know, the only way I'm going to find it out is if I actually call Danill. Sure, it might be two in the morning, but Danill works for a man who's heavily involved in organized crime. I'm sure he's awake. With my phone in my hand, I unlock it and scroll through my contacts. Eventually, I land on Danill's name and tap the small phone icon.

While the phone rings, I head into the kitchen and grab a bottle of wine from the fridge and a glass. It continues ringing while I'm opening the bottle, and finally, when I begin to pour, he answers. "Miss Amelia, what can I do for you?"

"Telling me what's going on with Ruslan would be a nice start." I know I probably sound a bit aggravated, but the truth is I'm worried. I'm worried because this man stuck his neck out for me, yes, but also because I've grown attached to him in a way I can't yet comprehend.

"I don't have anything to tell you. I'm waiting for Ruslan to contact me." Danill keeps his voice practically monotone. If that's not a surefire sign something's very wrong, I don't know what is.

"He was only supposed to be gone a few days, Danill. This can't be all you say to me. What are you doing to find him?" I'm not stupid enough to think everything's okay. I stop pouring my glass of wine and take a sip while I await some sort of response. The hints of cherry and wood float against my tastebuds, and I'd kill for some cheese right now.

"I'm working with his family to find him, Miss Amelia. So far, we only have a few leads."

"It's been weeks. You guys have to be close to finding him. Do you even know where he was going or what he was doing when he left?" I down the glass of wine after I finish speaking. I'm too stressed about this. Ruslan needs to come back because it's what he said he'd do. For some pathetic reason, I think he's going to follow through with every promise he's made to me. I'm only giving myself the opportunity to be let down again, but I need to have some sliver of hope that not everyone is awful.

"I can't discuss this with you, Miss Amelia. I can assure you I'm working as hard as I can, within my limitations, to find Ruslan."

Limitations? What the hell is that supposed to mean?

"What exactly are these limitations you speak of?" I question, practically barking it at him.

He sucks in a sharp breath, and there's a moment of silence before he speaks. "I was instructed to stay behind and keep you safe. It's why I'm still in Atlanta."

You've got to be kidding me. "You don't need to be here with me. You need to find him!" I snap.

"Believe me, if I could do it while killing two birds with one stone, then I would."

A bright idea flashes across my mind. "I have it. Take me with you. Then you can keep me safe, and we can try to find Ruslan."

"That wouldn't be a good idea," Danill laughs lowly, making me feel like a child who's speaking to their father.

"It's the only option on the table, isn't it? After all, you're not really going out and doing anything to help Ruslan the way things look right now." I don't care that I'm being a total asshole. I care about Ruslan, and I want to make sure he's okay. If Danill cares one bit about his boss, he'll end up giving in, and we'll both soon be on our way.

"Miss Amelia, you don't know the stakes at play here. Things aren't so simple. I cannot act brashly nor allow the fit you're throwing to influence me in any way," Danill comments, still in the fatherly tone I'm learning to loathe so much.

"At least I'm suggesting something! I'm not sitting around on my ass, not doing a damn thing!" I yell into the phone and hang up. My nostrils flare, and I pour myself another glass of wine. Just like the last, I take it down quickly. Wine calms me down, but I don't think it's helping me calm down today. Then again, maybe this entire situation is making me want to yank my hair out.

I can only keep myself busy so much, and working three nights at Illusion isn't enough to keep my mind from wandering. All I can think about the rest of the week is what the hell's going on with Ruslan. I try to keep my mind occupied as much as I can, so I overly clean the apartment I share with my cousin, and when she has tests, I help her study. It preoccupies me for a while, but not nearly long enough.

I leave the glass of wine on the kitchen counter and walk down the hallway leading to my and Emily's rooms. I go to her bedroom door and knock, needing to talk to someone about this. "Em? Are you awake?" Just as I ask, I realize I didn't see her car parked out front. Fuck, it's Saturday night. Of course, she's not home yet.

Emily's constantly doing stuff for school, and when she isn't doing that, she's working. Her only day off every week is Sunday, so a lot of the time, she'll go out on Saturday nights. It's a rarity that I'm home before she is.

In times like this, I wish I could talk to my mother. But we don't have a great relationship now. We did when I was a little girl, too young to realize what was right and what was wrong. But as an adult, I see her for who she really is: a greedy, manipulative woman.

My father died and listed my mother and me as beneficiaries on his life insurance policy. We both got a good bit of money, and within a year, my mother had blown through hers. She'd call me and beg to borrow some, and when I said no, she'd tell me I was selfish and ungrateful. I wasn't, but I wouldn't allow her to put a dent in my life savings. The identity theft issues started shortly after, so I guess the joke's on me.

I turn and head back down the hallway, only to see Emily opening the front door. Her dark brunette locks complement her entire outfit. She's in a skin-tight sapphire blue bandeau dress, and her hair's in a high ponytail. She has a deep charcoal smokey eye, and her lips are painted a peachy color. She looks so beautiful.

"You okay?" Emily questions with her brows furrowed. Her facial expression shows me she knows I'm not okay right now.

"I'm stressed. Stressed out of every orifice I have, honestly." I sigh and continue into the living room. I plop on the white couch, and Emily kicks off her heels, then proceeds to take a seat next to me.

"You wanna talk about it, or is it the kind of stressed where you just want to be distracted from all your problems?"

I throw my head back on the couch and bluster a sigh. "Honestly, I don't know."

I don't know much right now, but I know Ruslan isn't like anyone else I've ever met. He's a man of his word. He has to be.

Chapter Two

Ruslan

Lights shine above my head, but they're so bright I can't see anything else. The smell of bleach is in the air, and both my nostrils and eyes sting. Fuck, what's going on? I try to move my neck, but I can't. I thrash against something and then realize I'm strapped down. Not just my neck, but my arms and legs too.

Then it hits me all at once: the pain.

It spreads across my stomach, up and down my limbs, feeling like I'm on fire. The pain gets worse, and a tugging sensation causes me to scream. It's in the center of me, and I try to see what's going on. All I'm met with is the bright lights and the color red. The pain worsens, and people speak in the background with panicked voices, but I can't make out what they're saying. The agony is drowning everything else out.

My body goes into fight or flight mode, so I thrash in a desperate attempt to get away, but it doesn't work. As I try to move, the pain gets worse, and the tugging sensation grows more intense. My screams drown everything else out, and I close my eyes, trying, praying, in fact, for this all to be over.

Out of nowhere, a pair of hands press on my chest, and there's an impact against the side of my cheek. "Shut the fuck up, you stupid idiot!" a man's voice I don't recognize tells me.

"Fuck, he's being too loud. We need to kill him and stop this madness," another man speaks up.

"We can't kill him. You know this, so why do you speak like you don't?"

"Yeah, well, I didn't expect him to be this much of a fucking problem. Why did we even agree to this? We didn't get paid enough for this shit, boss," the man who suggested they kill me says.

"Of course, he'd be a fucking problem! He's an Umarova, for fuck's sake. Yes, our options are limited, but we will deal with him to the best of our ability, just as we deal with all the others," the original man tells the other, and for a moment, there's silence.

I find myself focusing on what they're saying, trying not to think about the pain that isn't ceasing. Nausea courses through me, and the tugging sensation continues. It gets worse by the moment, and I begin thrashing again. It's a natural response. I have to keep moving. My heart thuds inside my chest, pounding so intensely that I feel it in the center of my head. Fuck, when will this stop?

All of a sudden, a crashing sound overrides all the other noises in the room. "What the fuck is wrong with you all?! We have a job to do, and thus we will do it! Anzor entrusted us to do this for him, and we won't fail to do as he's asked. If we do, I'm sure you all can figure out what he will do to us." This is the old man's voice from the shack. No one says a thing after he speaks. I'm sure they're all processing what he said, but so am I.

I suspected my stepfather had something to do with this, but I got it straight from the horse's mouth. The confirmation I was so desperately seeking. That bastard did this.

He fucking did this.

I open my eyes for a moment, and the old man's peering over me, holding a syringe. "This should get you to shut up for a while." I'm stuck in the neck again, and a few moments later, darkness surrounds me.

※

I wake up in so much pain I vomit. I'm strapped down to the bed at my wrists and my ankles, but I have enough room to throw up over the side of the bed and not on my sheets. My head pounds, and I highly doubt they gave me any painkillers. The same agony I felt hours ago courses through me in waves, mainly focused in the center of my stomach.

The room I'm in isn't anything spectacular. It looks like it's cinderblock, and the floor is cement. I bring my right hand up as high as I can get it, and I attempt to bend. My stomach curls, and the pain only grows worse, but I don't care. I have to try to get out of here, even if I feel like I'm dying in the process.

The door to the room opens, and the old man presents himself once again. He runs a hand along his brittle beard and shakes his head. "I thought maybe you'd learn after the first time, but alas, you have not."

"What can I say? I'm a stubborn bastard," my voice comes out in a crackling tone.

"No, foolish is what you are. You've been stabbed, and during surgery, you tried to escape. You could've bled out on the table, and now, here you are, trying to get out when we both know you won't make it very far."

"Maybe, maybe not. At least I'll have tried," I snap, anger evident in my voice. He has no idea what it's like to be in this fucking place. My stepfather broke every code our family had. He's no longer my family. He's public enemy number one.

"It'll only cause you more pain if you work against us." Like I have a choice? I know how this works. If I don't try to get out of here, I'll be tortured and eventually killed. Sure, they might not want to kill me yet, but there will be a time when they get the green light, and I'm not planning on sticking around long enough for that.

"What does it matter? All I know is pain," I roar at him at the top of my lungs. I don't care about typical pleasantries like respect or manners. "How much is he fucking paying you? I bet it's fickle because his pockets don't run deep."

"It was enough to secure the job," the old man tells me, his eyes trained on mine. He's a tough, old type, and our roles aside, I admire that in a man. It's hard to find people like this. People who will never stray from the task at hand.

"Anzor has nothing. Everything he does have is mine. It's the Umarova family's, and Anzor is not an Umarova, even if he tries so desperately to pretend to be one. So it seems I've paid you to do this to me, not him," I laugh because this is laughable. My stepfather is technically using my family's money, and I know it. He's been doing it for years, and I should've had his cards shut off when I threatened him. Looking back now, I would've done things so much differently.

"I don't appreciate what you're trying to do. It's sneaky, like a snake," the old man tells me.

"No, it's the damn truth. You don't like it because you know I'm fucking right," I hiss.

The old man pulls out a cigar from his suit jacket and pulls out the cutter for the cigar. He cuts the tip off at the end and lights it, then takes a few puffs. There's a dense silence between us, and he approaches me. Every step is calculated, and he comes within reach. The old man slides the cigar cutter over my left middle finger and closes it without hesitation.

"The thing is, Ruslan Umarova, I am not loyal to you, and I never will be."

Chapter Three

Amelia

It's been three days since I called Danill and gave him literal hell. I wish it were enough, but I haven't heard a damn thing from him. I've seen him parked outside my apartment complex, though. He's here every day, and when I drive to work at Illusion, he's behind me in the blacked-out SUV. Ruslan told him to keep an eye on me, and Ruslan doing that makes me feel like I must be special to him. Then again, I might not be special at all. It could simply be because of everything that happened at Illusion.

I walk over to my coffee pot, grab it, place it under the faucet, and fill it up to the eight-cup mark. I could kill this whole pot myself if I wanted, but I've really been trying to cut back. The extra caffeine makes me a bit more jittery, and I'm not trying to be overly stressed. I tilt the pot over the water tank and slowly pour it in, careful not to spill any water on the counter. As I proceed to get a clean filter and put coffee grounds in the top, all I can think about is Ruslan.

I remember how caught on every word I was when he promised he'd make the person who stole my identity pay for it.

"I can't fathom why anyone would hurt you. When you were dancing in that cage, I could tell there was something special about you, and I knew I was right. I am right. So, whoever attempted to ruin your life is going to pay with their own. That's why I'm doing this. That's why I make these promises and statements to you... because they

will pay greatly."

I was a fish hooked on the line when he told me all that. It was the first night I really felt myself becoming attracted to him. I remember how he kissed me after he said it and the feel of the cool chill of his gold chain as I wrapped a finger around it. He called me his *malen'kiy krolik,* and every time he did, butterflies soared through my stomach.

We can't give up on Ruslan. We have to find him. I press the start button for the coffee and turn around, huffing in the process.

"Okay, what is the matter with you? You didn't tell me the other night, and you're just getting moodier." Emily places her book on the kitchen table and rises from her seat.

I try to think for a moment how I could explain this to Emily, but it's so fucking complicated. "I'm frustrated with a couple of things in my life right now. They're not going according to plan, and I'm just pissed about it."

Emily raises both of her brows and stares at me like she knows I'm lying. "That sounds like a load of horse shit."

Well, because it is. I swallow hard and take a second to figure out how I'm going to tell her this. "I think you know I was *seeing* someone a couple weeks back." Seeing someone is the easiest way I can explain what Ruslan and I are. At least, what I think we are. I'm pretty sure we're dating, but he and I didn't put a label on anything. With our chemistry, it feels like we're officially together. Maybe whenever I see him again, we can have that much-needed adult conversation.

"I assumed you were, with the way you'd start daydreaming and all," Emily cackles, lightening the mood a tad.

"All right, well, I was seeing a man named Ruslan. About a month ago, he told me he had to go away for a business trip. He lives overseas but comes to Atlanta for work," I'm lying a bit, but I have to. Emily doesn't need to know everything I know about him. "He was only supposed to be gone for a few days. I figured he might be gone for two weeks at the most, just to give him some more time. Well, he never came back. I haven't heard from him since, and it's very unlike him."

Emily scrunches up her nose in annoyance, and I know what she's probably thinking. Ruslan ghosted me, and I'm being paranoid, ignoring the signs that are right in front of me.

"How do you know he's coming back?" Emily inquires.

"He said he'd come back."

Emily rolls her eyes and licks her lips. She doesn't say a thing yet, and I know she's trying to be as tender with me as she can. I've been through some intense shit throughout my life, and every now and again, I notice Emily metaphorically puts white gloves on before she speaks to me. I'm not as fragile and broken as she thinks I am.

"What if he only said that to keep you off his case, Amelia?" I know she's concerned, but she doesn't have all the information that I do.

"He didn't. Ruslan works in security and is very well known and respected. He left one of his colleagues here to keep an eye on me while he was away, and he's literally outside in the blacked-out SUV right now. I'm sure you can see it from the living room window if you want to look."

Emily's eyes widen, and she looks at me like I have a couple screws loose. "You're joking."

She rushes over to the living room window and pulls back the blinds, proceeding to look out through the window. The coffee maker beeps in the background, signaling it's done. I grab two mugs from the cupboard and make the coffee just as we both like it, creamy and sweet.

"I really thought you were fucking with me. No lie," Emily says, shaking her head in disbelief as she comes back into the kitchen.

"Yeah, I'm not. I called the guy out in the SUV the other day. I asked him point blank if he knew where Ruslan was, and he told me he didn't. I ended up getting enough information to figure out Ruslan told Danill, the dude in the SUV, to keep an eye on me. That's why Danill isn't out there trying to find Ruslan… because Ruslan gave him a job, and he knows better than to disobey him."

"Holy shit. You said well respected. I think you mean feared too. Employees who are terrified of their bosses act like that."

"Yeah, but Ruslan hasn't contacted him either, so I know he's in some sort of trouble."

"Okay, so what are you going to do about it?" Emily asks as I hand her one of the mugs of coffee.

I blow on the hot liquid before taking a sip. "I don't know, but I think I'll find out soon. Come on." I place the mug on the counter and head straight for the door. My hair's up in a messy bun, I have an oversized Metallica T-shirt on, and I'm in a pair of shorts. Basically, I look like a bum, but I want answers.

I'm out the door before Emily's even made an attempt to follow me. I walk straight up to where Danill's parked, and he slowly rolls down his window.

He cocks both of his brows up and pushes his thick sunglasses down the bridge of his nose. "How can I be of service, Miss Amelia?"

"What updates do you have for me?"

Danill laughs, but he isn't amused in the least bit. "I've been in communication with Ruslan's brother, Lom, who's handling the situation."

I wait for him to say something else, but that's all he tells me. "Seriously? That's all you have to tell me?"

"His brother is handling it. I have a job to do, which is making sure you stay safe and don't get yourself into too much trouble."

I lick my lips slowly and debate what I'm about to say, but I've decided to go full-on apeshit. I'll look crazy, but I really don't give a damn.

"If you don't figure out when we're on the next flight out of here, I'm going to hurt myself and tell Ruslan you didn't protect me. I'll tell him it's all your fault, and he'll believe me because he's fucking obsessed with me. He's like a kid, and I'm his favorite toy to play with. I'm tired of the lack of progress you're telling me, Danill, so get with the program or get your ass fired."

Very calmly, Danill replies like nothing I've said phases him. "If you think getting fired is what will happen to me, you're really out of your mind."

"Great, then you value your life. When are we all leaving?" I raise both of my brows, trying to show Danill I'm not giving up.

"We all?" Danill questions.

"Yeah, I'm bringing her with me." I point back to Emily, who's slowly coming down the sidewalk.

"No."

"I'm not asking for permission. She's coming too. She can keep an eye on me while you go out and bust your ass finding Ruslan. She'll keep me out of trouble." I smile at the end, trying to be a bit more convincing, but Danill doesn't buy it.

"Yeah, right," he says sarcastically.

"Nothing is keeping us Stateside, Danill. We're leaving. So do whatever you have to do to make sure we leave tonight. I'm not going to stay here while Ruslan could be hurt and need our help. And don't you dare tell me you haven't thought the worst. Obviously, nothing is okay. If it were okay, he'd be back by now. So save me the lecture and let's go find him."

Danill looks into my eyes and swallows. I know he wants to fight against me, to push back, but at the end of the day, I know he's worried about his friend slash boss. I'm worried, too, and the sooner we get this flight organized, the sooner we can leave. Hopefully, it'll mean we'll find Ruslan quicker too. I just pray he's still alive.

He's the only man who's ever made me feel worthy, and I don't want to lose that yet.

Chapter Four

Ruslan

Two Weeks Later

It's been two weeks since I had surgery. I know this because I've been staring out of the narrow window at the top of my room. Over my time here, I've discovered more small details. For example, it's made of cinderblock, yes, but there are cracks near the bottom of the structure. When it's very windy out, there's a draft that comes through the room.

The old man comes to visit me at least once a day, and it's usually when he brings me some pathetic excuse for a meal. He likes to taunt me with what the food was before he blended it up and made it into a porridge-like substance. Whenever he can, he makes sure I know this is what traitors get. I found it laughable at first how he calls me a traitor, but now I'm just so damned annoyed by it all.

He has the nerve to call *me* a traitor. It's pathetic, really. What he needs to do is look in the mirror. Anzor isn't an Umarova. He has no claim to the power my name holds. None!

The distinctive smell of cigar smoke wafts through the air, and I realize it must be that time of day. I wonder what type of food he'll have for me today. Blended livers, perhaps? I figure he probably gives me the things his dogs don't eat. The old man's told me how much he despises me. He also never fails to tell me I'm still alive because he was instructed not to kill me.

I'm still strapped down to the bed at my wrists and ankles, so I can't move even if I wanted to. Sure enough, the door leading to my room creaks, and he fills the doorframe. In his left hand, he's holding a bowl with a spoon. This is a first. Normally there's a straw. "You look extra aggravated today, Ruslan."

"Well, you chopped off one of my fingers and torture me every day. I'm not exactly glad to see you, old man." I still don't know his name, even with as much time as I've been here.

The old man smiles sinisterly and digs into his right pocket, pulling out the cigar cutter he used to amputate my finger. "Why, because of this little thing?" The little thing he uses every day to open my wound. He has his questionable doctors close the wound back up, then he cuts it open again, and it repeats back and forth. I doubt whether it'll ever stop. I could see it continuing for however long I am here.

Every few days, he goes to another finger and cuts it but doesn't amputate it. He really doesn't care if things aren't healed or not. I think he's betting on the fact some sort of infection will kill me, and then he won't be "responsible" for my death.

"How long will you keep me in this fucking place?" I haven't asked him this question since he amputated my finger. On that day after the amputation, I did, but I've learned not to speak to this man. He will use whatever I say as a way to punish me further, so I should expect some sort of pain or possibly lose another finger.

The old man sets the bowl on my lap and then tilts it over, definitely on purpose. "Oh, would you look at that? Tsk. I don't have anything else to give you."

I should know by now not to let anyone further aggravate me, but it's growing more difficult by the day. This man does whatever he can within his power to make my time here insufferable. Now he's taken my one meal a day away from me, and I already feel so weak. Over the last couple of weeks, I know I've lost weight. My once-muscular arms are anything but that these days. I've been strapped down to this bed so long that my ass fucking hurts. It's so bad I'm sure I have sores on my bottom or behind my thighs.

"You're a vile piece of shit," I tell the old man, and he cranes his neck to look at me. If I was the type of man who became intimidated easily, I'd say right about now is the time chills would run down my spine, and my stomach would be in knots. But I'm not. All I want to do is get out of these damn bindings and beat him bloody.

He swipes the bowl from my lap and tosses it to the other side of the room. It cracks against the cinderblock and busts into many pieces.

Footsteps head in our direction, and the door to the room is shoved open. "Boss, you good?"

The old man turns and looks at the man now occupying the doorway. "Yes, this idiot threw his food at the wall. Stupid of him, no?"

The man in the doorway glares at me and shakes his head. I wonder why the old man lied, why he insists I did something when we both know he did it. Is it because he has to keep his men in line? His men who very much want to go against him and kill me. Perhaps.

"You never answered my question," I tell the old man. I stare at him, not averting my gaze for a moment.

"And which question was that?" He knows exactly what it was, but he's fucking with me right now.

"How long do you plan on keeping me here?" I speak slowly, enunciating every word.

The old man loses his patience and comes charging at me. He grabs me by the dirty shirt I've been in since I've been captive and rears his fist back, clocking me directly in the face. A stinging sensation floods over the bridge of my nose and out either side, then I notice blood. Motherfucker.

"I will keep you here however long I want! I don't know why you think you're able to question me, but you're not. You are subjected to my rules and treatment. Don't you think it's best if you try and not piss me off for once?" The old man walks away from me and heads for the door.

"That would be hard to do, considering you hate that I'm here. I'm a traitor, remember?" I don't hold back my anger from the old man, and he charges at me once more. But he stops and rushes out of the room when a ruckus comes from around the door.

The hallway has to be packed to the brim because it sounds like things are falling off tables or the walls. For a few minutes, the commotion continues, and the old man comes back into the room. His nostrils are flaring, and his face is beet red. Something's obviously upset him.

Maybe this is it. Maybe this is when the cavalry has finally arrived. Then, I spot a familiar sight. My brother, Lom.

His expression is tight, and he keeps his lips in a firm line. Lom points his gun at the old man, and I know he's about to shoot him. "No, he's mine," I hiss at my brother, and so he goes up to the old man and smashes the back of the gun against his face. The old man stumbles to the ground, somehow still conscious. Lom hits him again, and finally, he passes out.

Lom comes over to the bed and begins unstrapping my ankles. "How did you find me?"

My brother cackles lightly. "I'm afraid you're not the only one with connections, brother."

"It took you long enough to find me," I poke fun at Lom, but there's a sense of seriousness in my voice. If he were in my position, I wouldn't have let him go a few days without finding him. So, why did it take so long for Lom to find me?

"You weren't exactly easy to find. They did a good job at keeping you tucked away and out of sight, but there's always someone who knows something. Come now. We can discuss this all later." Lom holds an arm out, and I take it. It's the first time I've stood in so long, and my legs feel like jelly. It's harder than I want to admit to support my own body weight, but I'm trying.

As Lom walks, I'm forcing my legs to move as quickly as he is, and he's doing a great job at keeping me upright. It has to be because of the lack of calories and water I've had. I know the people here have only been giving me the bare minimum to keep me alive. Nothing more.

Lom heads to the right, and there are men in suits who I know work for the family. We get to the end of the hall, and there's a doorway. Lom pushes it open, and we walk outside. God, the sunlight feels so good against my face. I doubted if I was ever going to feel it ever again.

I stare off into the distance and see blacked-out SUVs, no doubt owned by my family. Then I spot a familiar face. One I know should be back in Atlanta—Danill.

A car comes flying up to the location, and I know it's not one of ours. Four men exit the vehicle, and Lom wastes no time shooting them down one by one, not leaving any of them alive.

Danill approaches Lom and me. "That must be the last of them. The team's cleared out everyone else."

"Everyone except one. The old man in the building with the beard, bring him," I hoarsely instruct Danill, and he nods, heading for the building to do as I've ordered him. I'll find out why he's here soon enough, but first, I need a drink and something to eat.

Lom walks me up to the closest SUV and puts me in the passenger side. I revel in the feeling of luxury, the seats are so plush, but they're so hard as well. "We'll be getting out of here in just a few minutes, brother. All you have to do is wait a little longer."

"As long as you get me a cool drink and something to eat, I don't care how long you take. Do as much as you'd like." I wave my brother off, and he cackles, probably because of my mood. I have a lot of anger inside me, but Danill's getting the old man, and I can deal with him when I'm at my best again. Until then, I need to get strong and get back to my life.

Fuck, I don't even know how long it's been. Amelia's probably worried sick about me or thinks I abandoned her. I shake my head and then look at my brother. "How long has it been since I went missing, Lom?"

"About seven weeks. I'm sorry I couldn't find you sooner. They did a good job, and I just got help last week when Danill showed up."

"Danill showed up a week ago?"

"Yes, and he brought two women with him. One who's quite taken with you, I might add."

"Amelia." Saying her name causes a smile to tug at my lips. God, how I've missed her. "I need to get back to her."

"And you will. We have at least a ten-hour drive back home, and once we get there, we'll get a doctor to look you over. I want to make sure you don't get any infections from these." Lom points to my hands where the old man had cut me.

"Well, I'm not dead yet. I'm sure infection would've settled in by now."

"Still, I'm not taking any chances. I promised the woman I'd get you back safe and sound, and I plan on making sure you stay alive once I get you back to her."

Chapter Five

Amelia

For the entire day, I feel my heart pounding in my head. Danill, Lom, and their team of men finally got a lead yesterday on Ruslan's whereabouts, and they left during the middle of last night. They wouldn't tell me much, but Danill did say they had around a ten-hour drive to find out if this was where Ruslan was being held.

It's been almost twenty-two hours since then, and I'm growing more aggravated by the moment. I pull out my cell phone and shoot a text off to Danill.

To: Danill

Well? What's going on? I haven't heard from you. You're making me think you're all dead.

I stare at the screen waiting for the three little dots to pop up, but they don't. Tossing my phone on the couch across from me, I slump back against the cushions and let out an aggravated huff.

"Moaning and groaning won't help, you know. Danill went with Ruslan's brother and that whole team. I'm sure they're fine, and I'm sure they're on their way back right now." Emily's doing her best to make me feel better about this whole situation, but how can I feel any better when I'm worried sick!

"One thing I'm learning through this whole experience is how things never go the way we expect them to. They found a lead, yeah, but they don't know that's where Ruslan is. If it is, what's to say Ruslan's even alive? He could've been dead for weeks by now." The mere thought is enough to cause nausea to roll through me. I don't want to even think about it.

"Stop thinking so negatively! You don't know he's dead, so why are you forcing yourself to accept a reality you don't even know is real? You're torturing yourself, Amelia." Emily points out, and tears come to the surface.

I rub the back of my fingers against my eyes in an attempt to wipe them away. "I think I'm trying to tell myself the worst has happened, so it doesn't break my heart when they tell me he's gone."

Emily gets up from the couch where I threw my phone and comes over to sit next to me. She wraps her arms around me in a hug and holds me tight. "From what you've told me about Ruslan, he's a force to be reckoned with. There's no way in hell someone has killed him because he simply wouldn't allow it." I haven't told Emily everything, but since we've been in Chechnya for the last week, I've let my guard down a bit more and have told her other things about my relationship with Ruslan.

"You know, it's crazy. At least it makes me feel that way. I wasn't looking for anything, and I certainly didn't want another man to come walking into my life when he did, but he came crashing down every door along the way, and now I can't imagine it without him." I feel like some lovestruck woman in a romance novel. I mean, what do I really know about Ruslan besides the fact he's rich, involved in crime, and wants to take care of me? Nothing, that's what.

"I'm certain he's as infatuated with you as much as you are with him, and when he comes through that door in a bit, you're going to see so for yourself." Lord almighty. How is Emily being so damn positive?

"You're just Miss Jolly today, aren't you? Should I go to bed with my pajamas inside out for good luck too? I've been left in the dark by Danill and Lom, and you're acting as if everything's perfectly fine."

Emily releases me and throws her head back in laughter. "I can't tell you why they haven't texted you to let you know what's going on, but I can say I have a good feeling about how today's going to go. You're either going to trust it, or you aren't, but that's not on me. It's been—"

"Twenty-two hours, I know," I interrupt her, and Emily's eyes widen.

"They know what they're doing, Amelia. They have a grasp on the situation, and they're dealing with it. Fuck, have you been counting every minute?" she's asking me in a half-serious, half-joking way… but the kicker is I have been.

"I'm anxiously awaiting their return. What do you think?"

Emily looks at me sternly and grabs ahold of my hands. "Amelia, I love you to death. You're the best cousin I've ever had, and I need you to trust me. The man put his head on the line and paid a debt you were set to take the fall for. He's coming back to you. A man like that doesn't just disappear off the face of the Earth or die tragically. They always come back to the woman who makes their heart flutter."

Okay, I'm really starting to feel like I'm living my life in a romance novel right about now. Emily gets an A+ for her positive, uplifting, supportive character. "Maybe when he walks through that door, and I see him for myself, I'll feel so much better about everything. Until then, let me be an anxious mess. I should have more information by now. It's not like Danill doesn't have my number or anything."

"You'll know more as soon as you can. Trust in that. They might not be texting or calling you right now because they can't. It could be dangerous or something." Emily shrugs, and I wish it were true. She clears her throat just as I think she's finished speaking and adds more, "I know you're head over heels for the guy, Amelia, so give him some time to come back to you."

"All I want is for him to be okay," I mutter, and tears threaten to come out again. I wipe my eyes and breathe in slowly through my nose.

Just as I finish speaking, the elaborate door from the floor below us opens. Lom told us Ruslan's house is at least two hundred years old and has endured so much. From the overall look of the place, anyone could tell it's historic. With all the woodwork inside and the stonework on the exterior, you'd be dumb to think it's a new development.

I jump up from the couch and rush over to the railing. Ruslan's house has three levels plus a rooftop terrace. The first level is where the front door is, and it goes directly out onto the street. Off to the right of the foyer area is the kitchen, and there's a study to the left with elaborate built-in bookshelves. Next to the study is the grand staircase that leads to the second floor, but behind the kitchen is a dining room, and off to the left of that is a vast living room. For being in the city, Ruslan has a large garden, which has a heated, inground pool in the back. The pool isn't overly large, but it could fit at least fifteen to twenty people in it easily. I'm sure he had it added for days when he wanted to relax from all the chaos in his life.

Sure enough, Danill comes in first, with his broad shoulders taking up most of the door, which says a lot since the door is rather large. Next comes Lom, with Ruslan at his side. God, he's lost so much weight, and his beard is now unkempt and unruly.

I dart down the stairwell, and Emily's bare feet tap against the hardwood floors behind me. "Ruslan," I say his name, but it comes out so desperate. Or maybe it isn't desperate. Maybe it's a sense of longing I've never felt before.

Tears fill my eyes once more at the sight of him. "*Malen'kiy krolik*." Hearing him call me by my nickname causes butterflies to soar in my stomach. I'm so ready to see him, wrap my arms around him, and hold him close.

Now that I have a good look at him, I see other things, like one of his fingers has been amputated above the knuckle, and he has cuts all over the rest of his fingers. His nose is slightly crooked, and there are dark, deep circles underneath his eyes. Ruslan waves his hand at his brother, and Lom reluctantly lets go.

For a moment, I stand and stare at him, but I can't keep staring here. I need to go to him. I break the distance between the two of us and rush up to him, but he holds out a finger. "At least let me shower before I touch you. I'm filthy, *malen'kiy krolik*."

"I don't care how filthy you are, Ruslan." I shake my head, letting him know I have every intention of touching him. So I continue forward and wrap my arms around him, holding him tighter than I ever have. Ruslan buries his face in my hair and breathes in deeply, a sure sign of relief.

"If this is a dream, it's not one I want to wake from."

"It isn't a dream, Ruslan. This is real. I am real," I tell him as tears flood down my cheeks. I was so afraid they'd be coming back with a body. I was terrified I'd never see this incredible man who makes me feel like I'm actually living. Before, I always felt like I was churning through life. It didn't feel like I was here in the present moment, and now that I have a taste of it, I don't want to let it go.

Ruslan takes his head away from my hair and presses his lips to the top of my forehead. "I thought of you every day. You were the only thing that kept me sane, Amelia."

I glance up at him and see he's speaking so honestly. He wouldn't dare lie to me, not after everything we've both been through. "I had to nag the fuck out of Danill. It turns out he really doesn't like disobeying your direct orders, so I came up with a compromise I thought was fitting."

Ruslan laughs. "Danill told me all about how you steamrolled him into getting you and your cousin a flight out here. You are a spitfire, my Amelia."

"Nothing was being done, and I was tired of being in the States with no progress. I figured if we all came here, Danill could do more, and I was right." I smile brightly, and Ruslan kisses my forehead once again.

"I need a shower. A doctor will be here in an hour to look me over, give me antibiotics, and whatever else he deems necessary."

"Okay, do you want help?" I ask, not meaning it in a sexual manner, but the men around us find it amusing.

"Yes, I need you to scrub my back, actually. I don't want to have a bit of oil or grime on me from that place," Ruslan grumbles and wraps an arm over my shoulders.

I help Ruslan up the stairwell until we reach his bedroom. Lom told me to sleep in here since I was *with* Ruslan, so it's what I've been doing. The bed isn't made, and the sheets are crumpled up from where I've been sleeping. Instead of being aggravated by the sight, Ruslan smiles. "I bet the sheets smell like you."

"Probably. Is that okay?"

"It's more than okay, Amelia."

I walk with him into the bathroom and help him get out of his clothes. Everything he's in is going in the trash. He stands there before me, naked and filled with dirt, grime, and oil. "Go in the third drawer on the right-hand side." I do as he asks, and there's a pair of trimmers. I plug them in, and he tries to take them from me, but his hands are shaky.

I place my hand over the trimmers and look at him directly in the eyes. "No, why don't you let me? I have a steady hand, and as long as you tell me how you want it, I can make sure it's the way you like it." I smile softly at Ruslan, and he nods.

"Fine, but grab the purple attachment for it." I head back over to the drawer and find what he's talking about. I slide it on the top of the trimmer and then turn it on.

Ruslan proceeds to tell me how he wants his beard trimmed, so I do as he asks. I'm sure he'll want his hair done as well. I'll do whatever he needs because I'm so thankful he's standing in front of me. This could've ended so badly, and I know it.

Chapter Six

Ruslan

She is better than I deserve. I hadn't ever thought about it before, but right now, I see Amelia for the genuine woman she is. She takes such time going over my beard, making sure it's exactly the way I've asked her to do it. She even has me look in the mirror in case she's doing something wrong, but she doesn't do anything wrong. It's perfectly done, just as I knew she'd do it.

After my beard, Amelia takes the trimmer over my hair, starting just above my right ear and then going over my entire head. She also has me check and make sure I like my haircut, but I do. It's perfect.

Amelia strips out of her clothes and turns on the shower, and I give it a couple of minutes before I step in with her. In the meantime, I take the liberty to brush my teeth for the first time in a month and a half. The more I've been standing on my own two feet, the easier it is to move around. I think my strength will come back in due time. I just have to move around a bit and slowly increase my calorie intake over the next couple of weeks.

Lom stopped at a local restaurant, and he told me to order whatever I wanted, but I knew better than to order anything heavy. I ordered oatmeal and orange juice. He thought it was a bland order, but it wasn't. Oatmeal and orange juice was a treat to me, given what I've been eating over the last several weeks.

I walk further into the spray of water, and the hot droplets hit my skin. It's as if I can feel the grime and oil cascading down my body. I stand there for a few minutes before her arms wrap around my waist and pull me back. She pulls me out of the direct stream of water and lathers my hair with the soap. It's a mixture of tea tree and eucalyptus oils with a bunch of others I can't remember. The shampoo burns my scalp, but it feels so good. After Amelia's done massaging the shampoo into my hair, I'm not sure if there will be any dirt or grime left. I have a beard shampoo on the same shelf, so she grabs that next, lathers some up in her hands, then works it against my beard. She rubs a little bit rougher now, and then we rinse off my hair and beard. My beard still feels a bit grimy, so I speak up. "My beard needs it again. It feels off."

Amelia nods and puts more of the beard shampoo on her hands. She comes back up to my beard, and I step closer into her space. Sure, she needs to be close to me for this, but I want her close in general. I want her sweet scent to waft around me. I tried to remember it to the best of my ability when I was in that wretched place, but since we're together again, there's no comparison. Vanilla and lavender fill the air between us, and I inhale deeply. God, it's so calming.

"Ruslan?" Amelia says in a concerned tone, which pulls me from my bliss.

"Yes?"

"You can rinse now. I think your beard is done."

I turn around, and the water hits my beard. I stand here for a few minutes while the water takes the suds from my hair. There's a conditioner on the shelf for my beard and for my hair, so I grab one and give her the other. Amelia puts conditioner in my beard as I put it on the top of my head, then I grab the scrub brush and get my pine tar soap. I rub the bar along my limbs and give her the brush to scrub. "I don't want to feel like I was in that place when we get out of here," I tell Amelia, and she nods.

She scrubs me with the brush, and the two of us continue our conversation. "You're not going to. You aren't there anymore, Ruslan. I can't imagine what it was like to be there, but I hope you can rest easy knowing you're no longer there. I…" Amelia pauses and looks over my entire body. "I hate what they did to you." She grabs the hand where I'm not missing a finger and holds it tightly. "I hate that you came back to me chopped up and sliced."

"Sliced and diced. They could sell me in a deli." I try to find some crude humor in the moment, but Amelia doesn't appreciate it.

"Why does your humor have to be so crass? Especially right now?" Amelia asks, scrubbing my back as she steps closer to me. She's never looked more beautiful. Half of her hair is soaked, while the rest of it's dry. Her tits are taut, and she has hard nipples. All I want is to feel her skin against mine. It's been too long, too fucking long.

I grab Amelia on either side of her face and pull her against me, crashing my lips against hers. She's surprised for a moment but eventually gives in to my advances. I'm sure she thought the first couple of nights would be slow and progressive. They're not going to be. I need her, and I need her right now.

My dick comes to life, and I was worried earlier that I wouldn't be able to get hard with the condition my body's in right now. "Rus… um, Ruslan," Amelia pulls her lips away from mine. "We shouldn't go too fast. There's no need to rush. You're back, and I'm not going anywhere."

"No. I haven't had you in weeks. You're the only thing that kept me alive in there, Amelia. I need you." As I finish speaking, Amelia collides her lips once more with my own, and then she tears them away out of nowhere. Amelia presses her hands against the tile shower and arches her back, giving me the perfect angle to hit her from behind. Fuck, yes.

Her pussy's shaved and glistening for me. I step behind her, and her warmth is inviting. If my hands were completely healed, I'd put a couple fingers inside of her and work her up quite a bit, but right now, it wouldn't be the best idea.

I line my cock up at her entrance and slowly force myself in. Fuck, it feels so good. Her wet walls constrict around my cock the further I go in, and I rock in and out of her. My legs begin to tense up, so I go a bit slower. I can't fuck her the way I want to because my body can't handle it, but I can let Amelia know how much I appreciate her.

I place my hands against her hips and hold onto her as I fuck her sweet and slow. She mews against the tile every time my cock is all the way inside her, and heat rushes through my body. "Fuck, *malen'kiy krolik*," I hiss right as I'm on the brink of release.

Amelia sinks down the wall a bit more and turns her head to look at me. "I want to see you when I come," she says, and I drill myself into her over and over again. I can't go too hard, but I can fuck her hard enough for us to both get what we need. She begins to moan louder and louder just as she's on the edge of her own release, and my balls tighten up, shooting my load inside her. Amelia comes around my cock and screams out. Her face contorts into pleasure mixed with exhaustion, and all I want to do is take her to bed after this shower, but the doctor will be here shortly, and I have to get checked out.

I help Amelia wash her hair and body, and we make sure I'm scrubbed clean before getting out. Amelia goes above and beyond, helping me dry off and fetching some clothes out of my closet for me. It's nothing special, but the cotton pajama set fits loosely, feeling cool against my now-clean skin. I told her I needed a suit, but she laughed and told me I was allowed to look like a "bum" for at least a few days after everything I'd been through.

Amelia and I head downstairs for a bit, and the doctor arrives ten minutes later. I undergo a complete checkup, including a blood draw. The doctor then tells me he's certain my nose is broken, so he's put me in a splint for the next couple of weeks. I'm supposed to go get an X-ray done at the end of the two weeks to see how things are healing, and then we can move from there. In the meantime, he gives me some painkillers and a course of antibiotics to take for the next ten days so we can make sure none of my wounds get infected. He, of course, tells me to keep them clean, and I'll have no problem doing that.

"Brother, do you mind if we speak privately?" Lom questions as he knocks on the door frame of the study.

"Of course not. Amelia, go get a snack and take it to the bedroom. I'll be up shortly to join you."

Amelia rises from the couch in front of the window and comes over to me. "All right, but try not to be too long. You heard the doctor say you need to rest."

"I won't be too long. Now go. I have things I need to handle." I'm not trying to be too dominating, but I need her to understand she can't be privy to this conversation.

Amelia walks out of the study and shuts the door behind her, leaving Lom and me alone. "Did the doctor say good things?"

Amelia was the only person in the room with me besides the doctor, so my brother had no idea what was said. "Yes, I'm to keep this splint on for two weeks, have a course of antibiotics, and the rest will be determined based on my blood test results. Otherwise, I was told to gradually adjust my diet to being back at home. Nothing too crazy, or I might get sick."

"So, you mean to tell me you've just survived hell, and you can't even eat a damn cheeseburger?"

"That would be correct," I laugh.

"Damn, that's fucked up."

"What is it you want to discuss? I don't want to stay down here too long, brother. Truthfully, I'm exhausted." My body's worn out from the long day of travel and all the moving around. I'm surprised I made it this long.

"I want to know what you found out while you were there," Lom tells me, and I realize he didn't have anything to say to me. It's the other way around. He wants to know what I can tell him so we can start on our own retribution.

"Anzor was behind everything," I plainly state, and Lom raises both of his brows.

"No," he shakes his head, wanting to believe our stepfather's a better person than he is, but it's the truth.

"I'm not lying to you, Lom. Anzor did this. Anzor was behind it all."

My brother goes to sit on the leather couch Amelia was on just a few minutes ago. "Deep down, I think I knew he must've been involved, but I didn't want to believe it."

"There won't be an ounce of mercy given to him for the things he's done. I need to know, brother, who is your connection? Who helped you find where I was?" Lom stills at my question and then opens a button on his suit jacket.

"The woman I'm currently sleeping with is Armenian. Truthfully, if not for her, I might never have been able to find you."

This is the first my brother's ever told me about a woman he's sleeping with. He's the drink and fuck type, then he usually leaves them hanging. "Is this woman important to you?" My question causes his eyes to widen, and then he laughs.

"No, not in the least bit."

"Then why are you telling me about her, and why is she warming your bed? You're too old for meaningless things, brother. Eventually, you're going to grow tired of being alone. I know I did."

"Yes, well, I'm not you. Plus, I'd rather focus on more pressing issues at hand than my love life. Anzor did this to you, and we need to find him."

I raise a brow and take a seat in my office chair. It's cushioned very well, but the seat is still hard against my skin. "What do you mean we have to find him?" I try to get comfortable, but after a few moments, I think I'm better off standing, so I rise.

"Anzor's been gone for a few weeks."

As my brother speaks, more things start making sense inside my mind. "Let me guess, for about the same amount of time I've been gone."

Lom nods.

To say I'm furious is a drastic understatement. Anzor lied to me time and time again. He took my family's name and power as his own when he's always been a fraud. What pisses me off even more is how my mother always turned a blind eye to it. She chose to do it. I didn't think she really understood what was going on years ago, but I think she knew exactly what was happening. She never did a damn thing about it, either. He clearly wanted power, and he did everything he could to get it.

"I don't understand how she never did a damn thing about it. She let him get away with all of this for years," I hiss, shaking my head. I bring my hand to the top of my hair and run my fingers through it.

"Are you talking about Mother?"

"Who else would I be talking about?" I don't mean to snap at Lom, but I do. I'm furious, and all this anger is eating away at me.

"You're allowed to be angry at someone, but it won't be her. I know you're furious. I can imagine why you're so angry, but Mother has nothing to do with this. So leave her out of it. She's only ever been concerned about our safety."

"Oh, so I'm supposed to believe she made every choice she has to keep us safe? That's laughable."

"She's our mother. Of course, she's done everything she could to keep us safe!"

"I've had enough. I'm not going to talk to you about this any longer. It's pointless, and I'm far too tired to go through this shit with you!" I roar and head for the study door. I pull it open and head up the stairwell.

The only thing I need to do right now is to be with Amelia. I've longed to hold her against my body for ages, and now I'll finally get the opportunity.

Chapter Seven

Amelia

Ruslan came to bed so angry the other night. He didn't want to talk about it, but I assume he got into some sort of spat with his brother. He and Lom haven't seen each other since the day he was rescued, but he told me this morning he's going to speak with Lom tomorrow before we leave Chechnya and head back home to the States. I didn't pry too much, but when I asked if everything was going to be okay, he told me it would. He said it had to do with an argument within the family, and they'd sort it out before we headed back to Atlanta.

Ruslan's been doing pretty well over the past few days, better than I thought he'd be doing. He likes to keep busy but isn't doing too much because he gets exhausted a lot sooner. It's to be expected for a while, I think.

When we woke up this morning, he insisted that we get out of the house. I tried to tell him it wouldn't kill us to stay in today, but he said it was our last day in Chechnya, and he wanted to show me some spectacular places before we left.

It's about midday now, and Ruslan had one of his people fetch an outfit he chose for me. It's a cherry-red dress with sleeves that go from my shoulder and stop at my upper arm, baring my shoulders. It kind of gives a cold-shoulder vibe, and I really like that about the dress. It stops just below my knees and complements my figure. I'm wearing a pair of black strappy heels with it, and it completes the look perfectly.

I head down the stairs into the foyer and find Emily chatting with Lom. Even though Lom and Ruslan haven't been seeing eye to eye, Lom's still been here. Personally, I think he's been very worried about his brother, and this is his way of making sure he's safe while he's home.

Redness shoots over Emily's cheeks as she laughs in a carefree manner, and then her eyes land on me. "You look amazing. Are you heading out?"

I nod. "Yeah, Ruslan wants to take me out on the town before we leave tomorrow."

Lom narrows his brows at me. "You're all leaving tomorrow?" Did he not know we were leaving?

"Yeah, I assumed Ruslan told you the other night?"

Lom's lips tighten, and he shakes his head. "No, I'm afraid not. I appreciate you letting me know." I wasn't trying to let Lom know anything. The last thing I want to do is get caught up in some family drama.

Footsteps against the wooden floors cause me to look up, and Ruslan's now coming down the stairs. "Are you ready for our date?"

I can't help but smile at his question. I'm so ready for our date—beyond ready for it, really. "Yes," is all I tell him because I don't want to seem like some excited, giddy schoolgirl. I'm sure before me, he's always had women falling at his feet, but I've never been that type of woman with him. I've found a backbone while being with Ruslan. A backbone I didn't have with my ex, Carter.

Ruslan approaches me, still moving a bit slower than usual, and takes my hand in his. A warm feeling rushes over me, and I revel in it. This isn't something I ever felt with Carter. Most of the time, I found I wanted to pull my hand away from his grasp. With Ruslan, it couldn't be more different. With him, I feel safe and protected.

"We'll see you all later," Ruslan tells my cousin and his brother, and we proceed to walk out the front door. I expect there's going to be some sort of SUV on the street waiting for us, but there isn't.

Ruslan tugs me to the left, and I continue walking with him. We continue for a block before I speak up and ask him what the hell we're doing. "Are we not getting a car to take us?"

He laughs and shakes his head. "No, not at all. Where I'm taking you isn't too far away, and a walk makes it more romantic, no?"

I smile at his question and step closer to him. I love how we can do this, walking so simply hand-in-hand. We continue for another block and then cross the street, and I think I know where Ruslan's taking me. It looks like some sort of park with all these structures constructed of flowers. There are hearts in a long row, maybe ten or eleven of them filled with red flowers. I don't think they're roses, but until we get closer, I won't know for sure.

Next to the row of hearts is a giraffe and two elephants made up of shrubs. Whoever does the landscaping here does a magnificent job, that's for damn sure. I don't think we have any places like this in Atlanta, but if we do, I now want to go to them too.

High-rise buildings fill the background of the botanical garden, and I quickly realize how cultured Grozny is. As I look over the gardens, many colors fill the scenery. From red to white, blue to purple, and pink to orange, the garden is vast and gorgeous.

"This is beautiful."

"Yes, it's one of my favorite places to visit in all of Grozny. Exquisite, no?"

He leads me under the row of hearts, and we walk slowly, simply taking in the moment. There's hardly anyone here, and it gives us a sense of privacy, which is lovely.

"It's unlike anything I've ever seen before," I comment, and I look over to Ruslan, who is physically here with me, but his mind seems so occupied since he's been back. I clear my throat and debate questioning him, but I have to be true to myself. Yes, he's been through so much over the last several weeks, but if this is going to work between us, then we both have to communicate honestly. "Ruslan?"

He turns his head to look at me and raises his brow. "Yes?"

"Are you okay? I... I haven't asked you yet, but you seem off."

Ruslan immediately forces a smile, and I'm sure he thinks I don't know he's forcing one, but he is. "Nothing could ever break me down. I'm not weak and fickle, Amelia." He speaks with such seriousness near the end, and I wonder if he believes I think he's weak. I don't.

"I didn't say you were. I know you're anything but either of those, but there isn't any shame in speaking about your feelings. You taught me that, Ruslan, and I'm a better person because of it."

"I assure you. I am fine. There's nothing we need to discuss." I know he isn't being honest with me, but I doubt he's truly being honest with himself. I imagine when you come out of something like Ruslan did, all you want to do is think that the world is normal, and you didn't go through hell to return to it. I won't press him for more right now, but eventually, we'll have to talk about this.

"Okay, well, did you notice how your brother and Emily were staring at each other when you came downstairs?" I question Ruslan, and he smirks.

"I did, actually. It seems my brother might be a bit taken with your cousin. Then again, pretty women seem to distract Lom easily."

"Is he bad news? Should I warn her not to get attached or be flirty with him?"

Ruslan tugs me closer against him. "She's a big girl, Amelia. I'm sure your cousin is intelligent enough to make decisions for herself. If she wants to get into something with my brother, then that's on her. I'm sure they'll speak about their arrangement before going fully into it, just as we did."

I raise both of my brows and laugh hard. "Our arrangement was very different, I assure you."

"Yes, but good in the end." Ruslan's voice comes out as smooth as melted chocolate, and he turns his body, so he's standing in front of me. Very delicately, he brings his lips to mine and gives me the most sensual kiss of my life. I find myself wrapping my arms around his waist and holding on, not for any specific reason, but simply because I don't want to lose this moment. We're under the floral hearts, and it's gorgeous.

He's the first to pull away, and his smile is the biggest I've ever seen. "I don't know about you, but I'm starving. There are some food trucks parked on the other end of the park around this time of day. We should go see them. If they're not there, we'll head to a local café before our next stop."

"Next stop?" He's taking me somewhere else. This is crazy. Any other date I've been on has been to *Applebee's* and then back home.

"Yes, there's an observation deck where you can see all of Grozny. I want you to see it. I don't know the next time we'll be back here, so I want to experience all of this with you." There's a sense of sadness in his voice. I'm sure he doesn't know that I can tell. Why is he sad? It's not like he'll never come back to Grozny. It could just be our last trip for a little while.

"Ruslan, we'll be back here before you know it." I try to be as encouraging as I can, and Ruslan presses a kiss to my forehead.

We walk through the rest of the park before finding the food trucks. There are about seven of them here, and Ruslan walks me up to one where he knows everyone on the truck. He orders us *hingalsh*—a handheld dough pie stuffed with pumpkin and butter—and *siskal* or fried cornbread accompanied by *to-beram*, a sour cream-based sauce for dipping.

I was a bit worried about trying such local foods when I first came to Grozny, but Lom's had practically all Chechen food for us at Ruslan's house. I have to admit, it's really growing on me.

Now we head for the observation deck, and I can't wait to see what I can only imagine is a beautiful image of Grozny.

Chapter Eight

Ruslan

I planned on speaking to my brother before we left for the airport, and I'm doing that now. I understand his love for our mother knows no bounds, and I, too, love our mother, but I refuse to ignore her indiscretions. She's chosen our stepfather over us, and it has never been more evident than over the last few months. Before, I believed it was there, but I think I ignored it. I chose to focus on other things, as my brother's been doing the last few days. He doesn't want to admit our mother has chosen a man over her children, but it's true.

"I think the two of us have calmed down enough to speak like adults," I tell my brother as we walk into my study. I round the desk and sit in the desk chair. The same desk chair that's a bit too firm for my liking, but I know over time, things will get easier.

"Perhaps we have, maybe we haven't. You're striking a chord with me, Ruslan. I don't like Anzor any more than you do, but I cannot stand you placing the blame on our mother too. She isn't him. She hasn't made the choices he has."

He has some nerve defending her, even now. "You have no idea what sort of choices she's made, brother. So, why do you speak as if you know what she's done unless there are things you aren't telling me?"

Lom's eyes go wide. "Of course not. I'm loyal to you as the head of the Umarova family. I know my place, Ruslan, and I'd be a fool to stray from it."

"Someone very recently told me they were loyal to the Umarova family too. Only, they weren't loyal to me," I hiss, and memories of the old man come to the forefront of my mind. How delusional did he have to be? He really thought my stepfather, Anzor, was in charge. In charge of a family that isn't even his! Thinking about it still makes my blood boil, and fire practically shoots from every orifice.

Lom sits down in the chair in front of my desk and stares at me coldly. "I'll make this very clear. I don't understand what was done to you there because you haven't told me about it. All I see are the marks on your body and the shape you came back to us in. I, for one, am not your enemy. I have never been, and I never will be. We will make those responsible for this suffer greatly, Ruslan. This I promise you."

Lom can make his promises, but what if things don't happen the way he wants them to? "What if our mother has some sort of involvement? What then?"

"Then I will do what needs to be done," Lom states clear as day.

"All right then, we need to go to the family estate. Just you and me. I need Danill to stay behind and keep the girls out of trouble."

Lom releases a low chortle. "With how spirited your Amelia is, I understand why you want Danill on her constantly."

"Yes, well, she's come a long way from the life she led before I was in it." Amelia was merely a victim before. She was a woman who got trampled on time and time again. She was used by friends and family and set up to take the fall for something I know she couldn't have ever done. It would eat away at her like maggots on a wound.

I rise from my chair because it's so damn uncomfortable, and we do have to be on our way. The flight we have booked leaves in three hours. All our unfinished business needs to be wrapped up by then. "Come on, let's go. I want to get this over with," I tell my brother, and he nods in agreement.

We walk out of my study and head for the street. Lom has blacked-out SUV parked along the street, and he unlocks it before we both get inside. He's in the driver's seat and pulls out onto the road after a few moments.

I grab my phone from my pocket and bring up Danill's name.

To: Danill

Lom and I will be back before we're set to leave. Watch over the women. Make sure they don't get into any trouble. If they want to go shopping before we leave, go ahead and take them. Use the card I gave you for whatever they want.

Danill's been working for me for many years now, and only last year I gave him access to an account I have for my travels. This way, when we get gas, food, or anything else related to being on the road, he has something quick and easy to use. The cash route grew old very quickly.

Within a short fifteen-minute ride, we're at our family's estate. It's vast and massive, but it should be, as it's the ancestral home of the Umarovas. Lom enters the code once we arrive at the iron gates, and they open within a moment. He pulls the car through, and we continue down the stone driveway that leads up to the impressive-looking house.

"Are you sure you're ready for this?" Lom asks, and instead of answering, I unbuckle my seatbelt and open the door. Of course, I'm ready for this. I'm ready for the fucking answers I deserve.

I walk straight up the stone stairs to the front door and don't even bother knocking. I place my hand on the knob and turn it, not surprised in the least bit when it budges without an issue. My shoes clack against the wood floors, and I head further into the home, scanning every room as I pass by. Sure enough, I find our mother in the living room, sitting in a chair that overlooks the back gardens.

She turns her head, and when her eyes land on me, she seems surprised. Her mouth falls open, and she clutches a fist to her chest before standing up. "Ruslan!" she begins to rush over to me, with tears already cascading down her face.

"Don't touch me until I have my answers," I seethe. Every bit of rage I've felt since this all happened is coming out. I'm the closest I've ever been to seeing the looks on their faces and if any of them knew what was going on. I'm not dumb enough to believe my stepfather did this alone. He had to have had some sort of help. I just don't know who helped him, and it's something I plan on finding out today.

"Answers? What answers are you looking for?" my mother questions me, drawing her brows together as she looks me over.

"He was told who was behind his capture, Mother," Lom fills her in, and she smiles brightly at the news.

"Good! Then you must make them pay for what they've done. Unless you've done so already?" she looks between Lom and me for confirmation.

"It's a bit more complicated than I'd like. I haven't found the man responsible yet, because he's been gone for almost as long as I have," I speak up, and I watch as she realizes what I'm insinuating. There's only one person she knows of who's been gone for about the same period of time that I have.

"You cannot be serious, Ruslan. You speak without saying everything, and yet I know what you are trying to say. But it cannot be true. It cannot be true in the least bit. Your father raised you! He would never do such a thing." She clasps the gold necklace around her neck, one I'm certain Anzor must have gifted her at some point in time.

"That man isn't my father. My father has been dead for a very long time. Have you forgotten Anzor's place? Have you forgotten Anzor isn't an Umarova, even though he walks around parading the power that belongs to my brother and me?" I scoff at the end and shake my head. She's as naïve as ever.

"He is the only father you've had for most of your life, Ruslan. He raised you! How could you believe he'd be behind this? He loves you!"

I slam my hand down on the coffee table beside me. "No, he doesn't. The only thing he loves is his power. The same power I told him I was taking away many weeks ago, or have you forgotten?"

"First of all, I think it's time you got to your fucking point. What was so dire that you needed us to be here tonight? Huh?" I snarl in his face.

His nostrils flare, and his fury is evident, but I couldn't care any less. "Release me, now."

"I'm done following orders from a man who doesn't have a leg to stand on in the Umarova family. You are nothing more than a glorified custodian. One whose reign has been up for quite some time. I've been more than accommodating to your dedication to the Umarova family, but the facts are very simple: you will no longer be running things."

"You can't do shit, boy," my stepfather hisses, and Lom cackles in the background, obviously finding this amusing.

"That's the thing, Ruslan can do whatever the fuck he wants, and he knows it. The person who has no power here is you, Anzor. You aren't an Umarova, and once we make sure all our allies know it, your words will mean nothing." Lom comes up beside me and snickers. "Now, what is it that's so important?"

Anzor grimaces in outrage, and I tighten my grip around his neck. "You two don't have any idea what you're doing."

Lom doesn't like to admit it, but even he recognizes how Anzor has used our name for his own gain. Though, Lom has a soft spot when it comes to our mother. I think it's because when our mother remarried, Lom was only four years old, whereas I was ten. I saw a lot more of what was happening while he was playing with his race cars and other toys.

"No, he wouldn't be responsible for such a thing. He loves you like you're his."

"No, he doesn't." I hiss, growing more aggravated by the moment. I know her love for Anzor knows no bounds, but he's used us—all of us—for far too long. Now, I don't think my mother is entirely innocent in all of this. What I think is that she didn't know how to handle everything when it was happening, and Anzor offered a helping hand. I know his hand wasn't helpful whatsoever, but my mother wouldn't have realized it any differently.

Out of the corner of my eye, I spot two figures coming our way, and I assume they're guards until the familiar faces of my half-brother, Nazyr, and half-sister, Eset, come into view. "What is all this commotion about?" Nazyr snaps, looking between Lom, me, and our mother.

"I could hear you from all the way in the attic," Eset adds. Eset is the baby of the family, just now reaching adulthood. The attic was turned into her art studio, where she could craft whatever creations were filling her mind. She's particularly good at textured paintings, but her oil paintings are also magnificent. "I'm glad to see you're home safe and sound, by the way," Eset adds and comes rushing over to me. She wraps her arms around my body, and I hold her close. She is definitely the baby of the family, the strong-willed sister filled with innocence and so much love.

I release my sister and look at her, then at Nazyr. "Your father's the one responsible for my capture and torture," I say as plainly as I can and await some sort of shock to roll through them, but my siblings don't even flinch at my accusation. Our mother, on the other hand, is an entirely different story.

"No! Anzor would not have done such a thing. Stop with this madness, Ruslan! Stop!"

I turn to face our mother and stare right into her eyes. "No, I won't! I was told firsthand they were loyal to Anzor. He instructed them not to kill me, Mother, but to keep me there for however long he deemed fit. If it weren't for Lom and Danill, I'd still be in that damned place in Armenia."

She shakes her head over and over again, not wanting to believe it. "He raised you, Ruslan. Why would he do something like this? He raised you. He's loved you as his own."

The more she tells me these things, the more I grow aggravated. "No, he didn't raise me. In fact, neither did you. Nannies raised me as well as the rest of us, or have you forgotten? You weren't there either unless it was a situation where it would've looked good for you to be the doting mother."

She rears her head back from the emotional hit I've dealt her, but I'm not done yet.

"All he's ever done is take what wasn't his, and I'm done with it. I warned him a few weeks ago his time as the head of the Umarova family was coming to an end, but now he has no idea what I'll do to him when I lay my hands on him. I would've shown mercy before, Mother, but now I will do no such thing."

"He's only ever wanted power, Mother," Eset speaks up, and my brothers look shocked at her admission.

"I cannot do this with any of you. He's your father, and you're speaking as if he's some traitor!" our mother cries, and she begins to walk down the hallway, trying to get away from us.

"Ruslan has never been one to lie. I'm sure you know that," Nazyr speaks up in my defense, and to say I'm shocked is an understatement. Yes, Eset and Nazyr are my siblings, but they're also Anzor's children. I never expected them to believe my accusations so easily, but I'm glad my siblings can see the truth their father has tried to hide for so long.

I even know Lom's aware of Anzor's true intentions. All Lom is concerned about is our mother, though. I commend him for his love for her, but she will have to fall in line like the rest of our family has.

Anzor is our enemy. He's an enemy who's been eating at our table.

⚜

Lom and I drove back to my home with our siblings on our side and our mother furious at us all. I've been trying to understand why she'd believe Anzor's innocent, but I have to remind myself she's been with this man for many years. She probably believes he can do no wrong and that he'd never go against the family. Personally, I think he's said these things to her over the years to truly make her believe he'd never do such a thing, but I know better. I know he'd do whatever he needed in order to keep the power he craves so badly.

It's ironic how all these things started happening a few short weeks after I told him I was taking the power that should've been mine in the first place. I don't believe in coincidences, but even if I did, I know this isn't one.

Before we got back to my house earlier, Lom told me he was going to stay here in Grozny for a while. He offered to handle things with the old man, and I agreed to it. He isn't going to kill him, but he'll torture him for as long as he can and gather information. After we both believe the old man has said everything he's going to say, then I might end his life, but only when I know there's nothing more of use to learn.

Amelia, Emily, Danill, and I all got on a private jet a few hours ago. If we had flown out commercial, we'd be forced to stop in Istanbul for a night and then head back to Atlanta. Over the years, the Grozny airport has had fewer and fewer one-way stops. Now, almost every time anyone takes a long flight, they must stop for an overnight layover.

The flight was long, but it was smooth. I got some good sleep on the flight, as did Amelia. When I first saw her after I was rescued, all I remembered was how beautiful she was. It had been so long since I'd seen her, and I didn't recognize the dark circles under her eyes or the way she looked so exhausted.

Now that I've had a few days to settle in, I see it, and I hope she was only unrested because of me being gone. She has no other reasons to not get good rest, and I'll hold her close to me every night if I have to. Above all else, I want to make sure she's okay. She has gone above and beyond my wildest expectations, and I promise to take care of her the way she's taking care of me. I doubt she even sees it, but I do, and I take note of it.

The plane landed about an hour ago, and we immediately headed back to the hotel suite I'd rented. I still have a bit of time left on the rental, but I plan to extend it for a couple more months. Eventually, I'd like to head back to Grozny, but there are things I need to tidy up here in Atlanta before that can happen. One of which is my meeting with Jordan Steele. He met with me a few weeks back to secure an arms deal. His supplier's run short as of late, and they need product they can sell and transport. We were supposed to arrange an official meeting to test the products, but my capture delayed said meeting. Since I'm back, I'll have to get that sorted.

"Ruslan, I'm going to take a shower. I'll be out in ten or fifteen minutes, okay?" Amelia says as she heads for the bathroom attached to the master bedroom.

"Take your time. We're in no rush, but I'd like to take you out in a couple of hours."

Amelia's lips curl upward, and she nods. "Okay, maybe I'll curl my hair then." She gives me a wink and walks out of sight.

My phone went missing when I was taken, so Danill got me a new one when we were in Grozny. I had it encrypted so no one could get access to the important information on it, but we have people who work with my family who can completely shut down phones. I had that done in the event it was given to my stepfather. The last thing I want him to know is what I'm up to or what plans I'm putting in motion.

I unlock my new phone and pull up Jordan Steele's contact. Amelia should be a little while, so this should give me some time to have a short conversation with Jordan. I tap the green call button and bring the phone to my ear. It rings a few times before he finally answers.

"Hello?"

"Jordan, it's Ruslan. I apologize for my delay." I'm unsure what I'm going to tell Jordan right now, but I debate telling him a good bit. The more allies I have on my side, the better.

"Apologies aren't necessary. I heard about your disappearance and am glad to hear from you. Are you back in Atlanta?"

"Yes, I am. I want to get our meeting back on schedule. We've had enough of a delay."

"Perfect. How about we schedule something for a few days from now? My schedule is a bit packed for the week, but this is a high priority for my family," Jordan tells me, and I imagine it is. Hopefully, he hasn't lost too much money due to my incapacitation.

"That sounds great. Text me with a date, time, and location when you're free. I'll make sure I'm there with the products," I tell Jordan, and we say our goodbyes.

Now all I want to do is go out with Amelia for a little bit. We both need to take in some familiar scenery, and Atlanta has been a lovely place to stay. Truthfully, I don't know if I'll want to go back to Grozny after this is all over.

Chapter Nine

Amelia

Ruslan and I had such a long flight home. I didn't think he'd want to do something after just getting back, so when he said he wanted to go back out, I was a bit surprised. Still, he's been cooped up for so long in that place. I can understand why he wants to get out of the house. There were probably times when he wondered if he would ever see daylight again.

I took a much-needed shower, blow-dried my hair, and even curled it like I told Ruslan I was going to do. I had some clothes here in his hotel suite because he told me to bring some a few weeks back just so I'd have something to change into. It's still a bit hot out, so I opt to wear a pair of shorts and a baby blue, sleeveless polka dot shirt. The curls I added to my hair shape my face beautifully, and I only put on a bit of makeup. I go a little heavy on the mascara, though, but that's okay. I really want my eyes to pop while I'm out with Ruslan.

I walk into the living area, and he's still in his suit. Why he insists on wearing them all the time is beyond me. The only time he wore something remotely comfortable was the day Lom and Danill brought him back home. Otherwise, he was in suit pants and a dress shirt.

"I'm ready to go whenever you are," I say to Ruslan, and he rises from the couch. I watch the way he stands and recall how he struggled the first couple of days he was back. Now, his strength is returning, and he's been eating heavier meals. I think he'll be back to his normal physique in no time.

"Then let's go. I don't want to do anything too crazy, but there's a park across the street, and I figured we could take a walk around it." It's obvious to me he wants to build his strength back as quickly as possible. I'm glad he includes me on these little walks. I think it's not only great for his activity level but also for the two of us to bond more.

"That sounds great," I tell him, and we walk toward the elevator. In about five minutes, we're outside, walking across the street, and Danill is in tow behind us. He's about forty feet in the rear, enough to step in if needed but not so close that he can hear every word we say.

Ruslan and I walk in the park for a few minutes in silence, simply taking in the scenery. The grass is the greenest I've ever seen, and flowers of many different colors cascade around the park. The path we walk on is made up of sand-colored cement, and it meanders all throughout the area. The paths even weave in and out of each other, so if someone wanted to walk up to the fountain in the center, they could.

On the outskirts of the park, they've added a track for runners. Some are by themselves with earphones in, while others are moms pushing strollers alongside their friends. Right about now, I revel in how peaceful it is being back home. For so long, I was terrified for Ruslan. But it was more than just fear for him. I had my own fears as well because without him, what would've become of me?

The truth is, I don't know. I'm not sure if the Steele family would automatically assume I had some sort of hand in Ruslan's disappearance, just as they originally thought I was the one to steal that money out of the safe during my interview. They could believe the common denominator is me, but I don't have to worry about those silly things. It doesn't matter at all because I'm here with Ruslan right now, and he's okay.

Ruslan wraps his arm around my waist and holds my hip firmly. It's something so small, but it shows me he's growing attached. I don't know if he realizes it yet, but I've grown quite fond of him as well. He terrified me in the beginning because of his nature and commitment to finding answers. I've learned that Ruslan isn't a monster I should fear. He's the monster in my corner, so others should fear him.

"Come sit with me for a few minutes," Ruslan says to break the silence, and just as he speaks, my phone starts to ring in my back pocket.

I fish my phone out and bring it to my ear without even looking at the caller ID. "Hello?"

"Amelia, are you able to work tonight? I know Britton was supposed to cover for you, but she's called out," Gregor, my boss at Illusion, tells me.

It's Friday night, so it's technically my night to work. Ruslan shouldn't have a problem with it, and even if he did, we'd be having a conversation about that. Our agreement was that I'd work Fridays through Sundays, and the rest of the week, I'd be his.

"Yeah, I can. Did she say if she's coming in tomorrow or Sunday for me?" Britton covered for me last weekend since I was away, and she was supposed to cover for me this weekend as well.

Gregor chuckles on the other end of the line, but it isn't an amused one. He sounds aggravated. "Yeah, she won't be in at all anymore. If you can work the next two nights, I'd appreciate it. And if you know of anyone who's looking for some extra, easy work, send them my way."

Immediately I think of Emily. She works during the day when she doesn't have classes, but every couple of weeks, she might want to make some extra money. I'll have to talk to her about it later.

"Okay, I'll mention it to a couple of friends," I tell Gregor, and we say our goodbyes.

Ruslan has cocked a brow and is waiting for me to explain what the conversation was about. "The woman I asked to cover me this weekend called out, so I have to go to work tonight. Gregor told me she won't be in tomorrow or Sunday night either, so I'll have to work those nights as well. He told me if I knew of anyone looking for some easy work to send them his way. I'm thinking about telling Emily. She's not exactly hurting for money, but the tips I get there are amazing."

"It would be a good idea to let her know. She's in college. That's why she's living with you, right?" Ruslan asks as we approach a bench in the park. The two of us sit down, and Ruslan moves his arm from around my waist to over my shoulder.

"Yeah, she's going for her master's degree. Her moving in is helping me with the rent, and I'm not living by myself, so I really like that." Ruslan smiles at my words, and he gives me a chaste kiss on the side of my head.

"I'm glad having your cousin so close to you makes you happy. I wanted to talk to you while we were out here today, more about what I do if you're open to it."

I give Ruslan a nod, encouraging him to go on, but he's silent for a few moments.

"I'm not going to sit here and tell you everything about what I do. It would put you at great risk, and it isn't something I'll ever be okay with. I'm also not going to sit here and lie to you or tell you I just work in security. You've become very important to me, Amelia, and my hope for us is that you'll be in my life for a long time to come. I've grown quite attached to you, and I can tell the same is true for you."

"I'm really attached to me, especially my body," I joke around with him, and he laughs, then shakes his head.

"I missed this humor of yours. It's refreshing to hear your silly jokes again." He rubs my arm and pauses for a moment. "My line of work is very dangerous, which I think you know now more than ever. My family is very powerful. My father's family, the Umarovas, have been in Grozny since the start of the Chechen Republic. My ancestors ran everything there, and nothing happened in all of Chechnya without them knowing about it. That being said, I think you've come to the understanding that my family is involved in the crime world. For the most part, I'm untouchable, but two people betrayed me as of late. One of whom I trusted for a very long time, while the other was someone I never really trusted all that much."

I don't know who Ruslan's speaking of, but I understand feeling betrayed. "I'm sorry you had to go through that. I… I hope you know you can always talk to me about these sorts of things. I might not understand completely, but I do understand quite a lot. My mother, in a way… she betrayed me. At least, it's how I think of it now. She just made really bad choices when I didn't do things the way she wanted me to."

"I wish your life was easier. I wish you didn't have to go through any of the things you did before I met you." Ruslan doesn't know every bit of information from my past, but he knows a lot of what's happened over the last couple of years. One day, I'm sure I'll tell him everything, but it'll all happen in due time. We both have pretty complex stories, I think.

"It made me stronger in the end," I offer a soft smile. It was shitty, but I made it through.

"You were already strong enough, to begin with, *malen'kiy krolik*," Ruslan comments lowly, and I grab the side of his face and pull him to me. I press my lips against his and kiss him softly, almost as passionately as he kissed me the other day. If someone had told me weeks ago that I'd be so content with Ruslan, I'd call them crazy. I never thought we'd be this close, not in the least bit.

I break our kiss, and Ruslan clears his throat. "I don't sell drugs, Amelia, but we sell other things. Things that are dangerous to a lot of people. If we're going to keep doing this, I need you to know how dangerous it really is being beside me, and I think you have some sort of understanding of the risks."

"I do. When you went missing, everything became very clear to me. I just…" I go quiet for a few moments, trying to think of a way to ask him this. "I don't know how to ask you, so I'm sorry if this seems so straightforward. Is your family the mafia or something?" I ask the last bit very lowly, almost so low that I can't really hear it.

Ruslan cackles, obviously amused by my nervousness. "That would be a good way to put it, yes." I notice Ruslan looks up, and he keeps staring straight ahead.

Sure enough, I look in the same direction and see a familiar face staring at us. One from my past that I never wanted to see ever again—my ex-boyfriend, Carter.

A sinking feeling forms in the pit of my stomach. It could be a coincidence that he's here. After all, he does live in Atlanta too. But before my mind gets too crazy, Carter walks off and is on his way. He must've just been in the same park as us. That's all it is. There's nothing more here.

Chapter Ten

Ruslan

Yesterday at the park, I recognized the man staring at us. The first night I went over to Amelia's apartment, I saw a photo of him with her. When I pointed it out, she threw it directly in the trash. She and I were sitting on that bench having a great time, but the moment I stared off into the distance and saw he was looking at us, tension immediately appeared.

I don't know a lot about their relationship, or lack thereof, I should say. But I know enough. I know he treated her like trash when they were dating, and I know that he packed up his bags and left the same day Amelia was accused of stealing the money from Christian Steele's safe at Illusion. Now, I don't believe in coincidences, so I think Carter has something to do with it. I just don't have any solid proof yet.

Amelia and I ended up leaving a few minutes after Carter walked off. I bought us some tacos from a cart at the corner of the park, and we went back to the hotel suite. She stayed there for a bit and then had to go to work, so Danill went with her, as he was supposed to do.

I caught a nap at the suite while she clocked in some hours at the club, and before I knew it, Danill and Amelia were back. Amelia didn't say much, but she muttered something about needing a shower because it was so hot in the club. I didn't think anything of it, so she went off and took another shower. Danill came up to me, though, and he told me a few things that happened over the night.

He said Amelia was acting very odd, constantly looking over her shoulder. He told me she was acting paranoid, like someone was watching her. Danill continued to tell me he questioned Amelia on it, and she didn't want to say anything to him at first, but eventually, she confessed that it felt like someone was watching her every move.

Now, Danill saw exactly what happened at the park yesterday with Carter because he was there too. Only, Danill was behind us, maybe forty or fifty feet away. When we were sitting at the bench, I think he was sitting a few benches down. I'd put money on it that Carter doesn't know Danill works for me or that it's his job to protect Amelia at all costs.

Danill told me Amelia said at one point in the night, she turned around quickly and saw someone staring, and when she tried to follow them, they disappeared into the crowd of people. It's obviously shaken her up quite a bit, especially with seeing Carter earlier in the day. Danill told Amelia she was safe with him, and nothing would ever happen to her while he was there. Apparently, she appreciated it but still seemed a bit upset with everything going on.

Now it's the next morning, and Amelia hasn't left to go back to her apartment yet. She wants to go get some more clothes, and I know she'll be heading out shortly. If I'm going to talk to her about it, I need to catch her before she leaves.

"Amelia," I call out in the suite, trying to figure out which room she's in. I continue calling her name until she finally calls back.

"I'm in the study," she says, and I head into the small office area within the suite. Sure enough, she's sitting on the chaise lounge chair and has a book open in front of her.

"What're you reading?"

She shrugs her shoulders and remains quiet.

"Is it some sort of secret or something?"

"Not quite. I'm just trying to understand more about identity theft victims and having some sort of hope. I've been so afraid my life is going to be ruined by this, so I'm just... reading this book about different people and their stories. Some of them made it through it and have amazing lives now."

"I'm going to take care of you, Amelia. You don't have to worry about your identity theft case. I'm handling everything, so you don't need to worry about a thing."

She releases a pent-up breath of air. "But don't I? I mean, all I've been doing is worrying since yesterday. Things just seem so weird, and the timing of it all is just... odd, I guess. I don't know. Maybe I'm looking into things too much."

"Why are you saying that?" I question her, raising my brow as I walk closer and take a seat in the chair across from the chaise.

"I haven't seen him in weeks. He was gone after that money was stolen from Illusion, then he just showed up at the park at the same time we were there. It's odd. It's weird. Then last night, when I was working, it felt like someone was watching me the entire time. Ruslan," Amelia pauses, puts the book down, and rubs her hands over her shoulders. "It felt so violating. I don't know how to describe it other than saying it this way, but I felt violated. I hated every bit of it, and I saw someone watching me. Then I tried to follow them through the crowd, but they disappeared. It... it makes me feel like someone's actually watching me, and sometimes I worry something like what happened to you could happen to me."

I rise from my seat and immediately move to the chaise, sitting alongside Amelia. I grab her hand and gently squeeze it, so she knows how serious I am. "Amelia, I will never let anything happen to you like that. It's why Danill is always with you because your safety is more important than my own. I can't focus if I don't know you're safe, so Danill being with you gives me that sense of security."

Amelia nods, and tears come to her eyes. "The truth is if I were in your shoes when you were taken… I don't know if I could've survived."

"I know without a doubt that you would've made it through. You're stronger than you realize, Amelia. So much stronger than you realize. But you'll never have to go through something like that. This I promise you. It's my job to keep you safe, and I take it very seriously."

Amelia sucks in a deep breath and nods a couple of times like she's trying to convince herself. I wrap my arms around her and pull her against my chest. She breathes in deep and slow, but they come out choppy and filled with emotion. "What if the person watching me is Carter?"

My muscles tighten hearing her ask me that. "Do you suspect it's him?"

"It could be, but I'm not sure."

Chances are, if Amelia thinks it's Carter, it probably is. I'll have Danill keep a closer eye on their surroundings. If it is Carter, it'll be no time before he's popping his head up again.

⚜

Amelia left with Danill, and they went to the apartment she shares with her cousin. I have been very busy over the last few hours speaking with my family's allies. It's been one call after the next with heads of families. I've spoken with Liam Mackenzie, who's at the top of the Irish food chain, and Alejandro Ramirez, the head of the Mexican Cartel. This was followed by Katya, who runs the Russian Bratva; Bianca Petran, the head of the Romanian Clans; the McDougalls, who run Scotland; and many others.

Right now, I have to reach out and make sure there's no question about who's in charge of the Umarova family, and it isn't my stepfather. All my allies have pledged their loyalty to me and not Anzor. At least, they've done so to my face. Who knows what they'll do behind my back. As much as I want to blindly trust all of them, I know better than to do it right now, especially with everything that's happened as of late.

Since everything's handled with my allies, I make a call to my brother, Lom. After a few rings, he finally answers. "Brother!"

"Lom, you sound a bit joyous today," I point out. In the background is the distinctive sound of city life. Cars whoosh by, and horns are being pressed left and right.

"I am, brother, that I am," Lom tells me, and out of nowhere, it sounds like the outside noise is dying down. "I moved to a quieter spot so I can hear you better."

"Perfect. How are things going with our old friend?"

"Well, actually. He told me Anzor's hiding out in the United States."

Really? I'll be damned.

"Did he say where?" If the old man gave him any sort of location, this could mean I'd be able to locate my stepfather a lot sooner than I thought I would. There's nothing more I want than to wrap my bare hands around his scrawny neck, not giving him an ounce of mercy. Then again, I don't want to kill him so quickly. I want him to suffer, and I want him to suffer greatly.

"It took a while, but yes, I was able to get that answer from him quickly enough," Lom's answer causes me to smile, and I'm anxiously awaiting what he's going to say. Though, I only wish I was the one to get the answers from him. He made my life hell for weeks, and in my opinion, he needs to suffer greatly for it.

"Don't keep me waiting." I lean back in my chair and stare at the ceiling while I wait for Lom to give me what I want. I notice a couple of spots on the ceiling where it looks like the water's coming through. I'll have to call the front desk and make them aware of it so they can send maintenance up to take a look. Hopefully, it's nothing serious. I've grown quite attached to this suite.

"He's in Boston," Lom finally tells me, and I immediately try to figure out why he'd be in Boston. It doesn't make sense to me because the O'Deas run Boston completely, and they fall in line under the Mackenzies, who are loyal to me. I know if any of my allies were going to turn against me, it wouldn't be the O'Deas. They're great allies to have and ones I'd never go against.

"Great, we can get deeper into that in a moment. I want to know what the stipulations the old man had with giving you this information." There's no way he would've given the info for free. When you're in positions like I was, you use what you can to grant your freedom. I tried using my checkbook, which the old man didn't take too kindly to. There was something more valuable there which was Anzor's whereabouts.

"He lost his damn mind, brother, that's what. He thought if he gave me the information we were looking for…" Lom pauses for a moment and lowers his voice to a mere whisper, "that I'd let him live. Can you believe it? It sounds ludicrous. Then he gave me what we were looking for, and it was so fucking easy."

Ah, so the old man finally understood what it was like to be in my shoes. Good. I only hope he suffered greater than I ever did.

"I do need to tell you something else, Ruslan," Lom pipes up, and I'm listening very closely.

"Go on."

"I found a photo of the old man with our father. It was old, in a photo album in storage. I kept thinking the old bastard looked so familiar, so I started digging through photographs. Sure enough, I found one."

"Why would our father be in a photograph with an Armenian?"

"I don't have the answer to that yet. But I am looking for some sort of answer for us."

"Good, he's still alive. You can press him for more answers and get more information. If his life is as valuable as he thinks, then he can give us more information."

There's a long moment of silence before Lom speaks, and I know I'm about to have a bomb dropped on me. "He isn't, Ruslan. I got the information we needed on Anzor's whereabouts, and then I ended him. Why the man was in a photograph with our father isn't a reason to keep him alive. I can find that information out somewhere else."

Every blood cell in my body starts to boil, and steam is coming from my ears. I'm certain of it. "Why in the actual fuck would you do something as stupid as that?" I snap at him, unable to control my rage. He found a photograph of the old man with our father and thought it would be a good idea to kill him. How stupid of him!

"It didn't seem important at the time. He hurt you, took your finger, scarred you. I wasn't letting him live."

"It wasn't your choice to make, Lom! You fucking know that! I'm the head of the family, not you. Sure, you hold some power as my second, but you are not the one who makes those decisions. Do I make myself clear?" I scream into the phone and decide I can't speak to him any longer. I hang up and rise to my feet, then throw the phone on the couch.

What was he thinking?

I understand he was probably mad because of me being captured, but there's no reason to kill someone when there's more valuable information we could've used. Lom fucked up today, and he fucked up incredibly.

I need to get my mind off my brother and his royal mistake, so I grab my phone from the couch and look up private investigators in the area. I won't hire anyone, but I want to make sure the person I do hire is exceptional at their job.

It's apparent to me that Amelia thinks this identity theft case is going to hang over her head forever, so I'm going to make sure it doesn't happen. No matter what it takes, I'm going to help her.

Chapter Eleven

Amelia

With everything that's happened over the last few days, I've been a bit shaken up. I find myself looking over my shoulder a lot, even after Ruslan and I spoke about it. He assured me I'd be safe, and I know he believes I will. I want to believe it too. I want to believe it so badly, but what if I'm not safe? What if Danill gets shot one day, and I'm taken?

I didn't use to think about these things before, but since I know what kind of work Ruslan's involved in and his family's status… everything has changed. I'm no longer so careless and confident. Now I'm much more aware of the dangers this life can bring. Add in the fact we ran into Carter at the park the other day, and I'm on edge. Then that night at work, I was being watched. It totally screwed with my head. I know it would mess with anyone, but still.

I've been keeping a low profile the last couple of days, mainly staying in Ruslan's suite at the hotel. He had maintenance from the hotel in his place doing some work yesterday, so Ruslan and Danill stayed with Emily and me at our apartment. Danill opted to sleep on the couch, and it looked hysterical. He's tall and lengthy, and the couch isn't very big. His legs were hanging off the end by a couple feet, so I sent Emily out to get the poor guy an air mattress. He seemed really happy with the choice when Emily came back with the improvised bed, a new pillow, and a blanket for him.

Come to think of it, without Emily, I don't know what I'd do. It's crazy how we just became close again when I was going through another rough patch. I don't really have any other friends, and I've noticed that throughout my life. I did when I was younger and when my dad was still alive. After he passed, things were much different. In a way, I think because my mother became so money hungry and greedy, I dropped a lot of people. I was afraid of them trying to do the same thing she was, so I isolated myself. It was a way to keep me safe, but it ended up hurting me in the long run.

Emily and I said we'd go out to get coffee together after her morning class, so I'm a couple miles away from her campus at a mom-and-pop coffee shop. It's called Rise N' Grind, and the inside is so homey and inviting. The floors are super simple, painted cement in a light gray, and the ceilings are wood. I don't know what type, but they're very narrow and long, with the stain of the wood ranging from dark espresso to bamboo.

The ordering station is off to the left, and it's made up of repurposed metal from barn roofs back in the early 1900s. I've seen enough farms on the outskirts of the city to recognize it. It looks just like the metal roofing on the old, abandoned ones. The display case is above the metal, stretching maybe twenty feet in an L shape. There's a glass wall about three feet high, so the food doesn't get breathed on.

They have fresh pastries like scones, muffins, donuts, bear claws, apple fritters, and so much more. Plus, they have a variety of breakfast burritos, deli sandwiches, soups, and freshly made salads. Emily told me this was one of her favorite places to get coffee, and I think I understand why.

On the wall behind the counter is their menu board, and it looks as if it's been made with thick, white chalk. The handwriting is a mixture of cursive and regular font, which gives it an eclectic feel.

"Hey lovely, what can I get started for you?" the blonde-haired woman behind the counter asks.

"Could I get one of those raspberry scones and a hot medium chai tea, please?"

She nods with excitement. "Of course. That'll be $5.74."

I hand the woman my card, and she inserts it into the chip reader. After a few moments, it flashes green, and I slide the card back into my wallet. "Your order number is 331. Will you be dining in today?"

"Yes, I will."

"Perfect. Pick any table number and let me know where you're at."

I scan over the options and decide on a booth next to the window. "Table eleven, please."

"Perfect. Me or one of my colleagues will bring it over when it's ready."

"Thanks so much," I say to her as I make my way over to the booth and have a seat.

I glance out the window and look onto the sidewalk, then the street. It's so busy around this part of town too. The hustle and bustle of the city never cease to amaze me. Cars pass by, and people walk with purpose to their destinations.

I spot movement from my right and notice Emily's waving her hand at me. She's in a cute plaid business suit sort of thing, and her hair falls down straight on both sides of her head. She has a pair of glasses on too, which is new.

"When did you get glasses?" I question her.

She giggles as she slides into the seat across from me. "Since I've been sending a certain Umarova brother sexy photos. They add a nice touch, don't you think?"

"You'd better be talking about Lom, or I might have to kill you." I'm totally playing around with her, but if anyone thought it was okay to come across to Ruslan in that manner, I would kill them very slowly. It's times like this that make me realize I'm in awe of Ruslan. He accepts me for everything that I am. He doesn't see me as weak, inferior, poor, or even damaged. He just sees me as Amelia.

"Obviously, I'm talking about Lom. He's a bit of a hottie." Emily smiles from ear to ear, and I know she's going to be in big trouble.

"What happened when we were in Grozny? Did the two of you get really close?" I inquire, and the woman behind the counter brings over my scone and my chai tea. She sits it down on the table and then walks off.

"I mean, as close as close can get, I guess. We flirted a lot. Had an intense make-out session, but it didn't go past that." Emily purses her lips out to the side like she wishes they did.

"What? Really?"

She furrows her brows and laughs. "Yeah, why? Did you and Ruslan make a bet or something?"

"No, but we should've. Shoot." I laugh and pick up my chai latte. The mug is nice and warm, so I blow on the liquid. The last thing I want to do is burn my mouth right now.

"You two play too much." Emily waves her hand in dismissal and laughs. "How're things at their hotel suite right now? Did they fix the leak?"

"I'm not sure, to be honest. Ruslan didn't say they'd have to stay at the apartment with us tonight, so I'm going to guess so."

"Okay, well, the hotel must work pretty quickly. I bet since Ruslan's rented it out for a hot minute that they're working quickly to appease him."

"Possibly. What did you end up getting? The entire menu looks delicious."

"I got an iced mocha with three extra pumps of chocolate and a tuna salad sandwich."

I instantly want to gag. Who mixes those two things?

"Fish and chocolate?" I make a barfing motion with my mouth.

"Hey! Don't knock it until you try it."

"I'd rather not, honestly." God, the mere thought of those two things together is enough to physically make me nauseous.

My heart sinks into my stomach, and I realize I haven't actively been looking for Danill. He has to be here because he's always following me. I scan the coffee shop in an effort to find him, but Emily cuts in.

She grabs my hand and bites her lip. "Amelia, what's going on with you? You look petrified."

"Um, I just realized I don't know where Danill is. I want to make sure he's here."

"He is. He's in the corner booth right near the door. I said hello to him when I walked inside." Emily takes a deep breath, and I realize she's the only person I didn't speak to about the park the other day and what happened at Illusion.

"Obviously, something's up, and I can tell you're seeing it."

"Yeah, I'd say. I've never seen you this scared in all our lives."

I release a bit of a sigh and look at Emily. "The day we got home, Ruslan and I went to the park across the street from the hotel. Not for anything specific, just to get out and take a stroll. Well, we were sitting on a bench having a really good conversation, and out of nowhere, I felt this yucky feeling. I don't know how else to describe it other than when you're somewhere, and you know someone's eyes are on you. That's how it felt. It felt like that."

"Okay… and?"

"It was Carter. He was in the park staring at me and Ruslan for God knows how long."

"Ew, that's weird," Emily comments, and the same blonde woman comes over with her tuna sandwich on toast and her iced mocha. Emily mutters thanks, and the woman goes off on her way.

"Yeah, not to mention creepy as fuck. I haven't seen him since the day that money was stolen at the club." I love the fact Emily and I have such an open relationship. It makes things so much easier. I don't think I'd ever be able to talk to anyone else the way I speak to Emily. Sure, I can talk to Ruslan about anything, but there's something about having girl time.

"Yeah, I bet. I just… I don't think you have anything to worry about, Amelia. Ruslan has Danill with you all the time, and I understand him working in private security can be super dangerous, but it seems like he totally has it covered." Emily doesn't really know what the Umarova family does, and I don't know if she ever will. I feel like that sort of knowledge is reserved for people dating or married to the Umarovas. I'm sure Lom's told her they work in private security as well.

"It wasn't just at the park, though, Em. I went to work that night. Gregor had called me and said the girl who was supposed to cover me called out. Long story short, when I got there, I ended up finding out she slept with one of the barbacks, who's married to another one of the waitresses. So, she wasn't coming back."

"Shit, that's horrible."

"Not as horrible as the black eye the husband had." I laugh, not feeling a bit sorry for him. No one should ever cheat on someone else. If you're not happy, then you shouldn't be in a relationship. It doesn't matter what the reasoning is. It does you and the person you're with a disservice. Not to mention, it's a huge slap in the face because your partner could deserve so much better than you.

"Good for her!" Emily cackles and takes a bite out of her sandwich. Seeing her take a bite reminds me I could take a bite, too, so I grab my scone and chomp into it. Scones are kind of like biscuits that are a little bit sweet. Not overly so, but just enough to curb a craving if you have one. "What's that have to do with your heebie-jeebies, though?"

"Shit, I got sidetracked. Anyway, while I was working the shift, I felt like I was being stared at the whole night. Sure enough, I saw someone staring at me, but I couldn't make out who it was. I tried following them, but I lost them in the crowd."

"Are you sure it wasn't just some random dude who thought you were hot or something?" Emily's question is good. I do get stared at frequently while working, but this was so much different.

"Yeah, this wasn't like that, Em." Deep in my gut, I think it could be someone who doesn't like Ruslan, but I won't know until we can actually find the dude. For fuck's sake, Ruslan was just rescued a little over a week and a half ago.

"I don't know. What I do know is that I have to go pee, so I'll be right back." Emily gets up from her seat and walks by the front door, but she stops where Danill's sitting and then proceeds to go to the restroom.

Sure enough, Danill grabs his coffee and walks over to my booth. He slides across from me, so he'll be sitting next to Emily when she comes back and cocks a brow. "Your cousin tells me you're being a bit paranoid."

"I'm not paranoid. I'm cautious. Those are two very different things."

"You know who says that?"

"No. Who?"

"Paranoid people."

Danill smiles at his own joke, and I roll my eyes. "I'm allowed to be a bit freaked out with everything that's gone on lately. It's a lot for someone to take."

"Yeah, it is, and I'm allowed to sit here and tell you to calm down because you'll be fine. The only reason Ruslan got into hot water was because he was an idiot who went by himself. If he'd had one of his brothers with him, I can guarantee you things would've gone very differently. Relax, Amelia. Try to have a good time with your cousin. Leave the worrying and over-analyzing to me. It's my job."

"Fine," I grumble and roll my eyes again. Danill gets up, takes his coffee, and walks back over to his booth. Sometimes I feel like he's being a father figure, and it sort of cracks me up.

Chapter Twelve

Ruslan

Today is the day when I can finally go and meet with Jordan. It's been a long time coming, and many things have come up between us, but it's great that we are finally able to get together. He sent me an address to a rural property north of Atlanta, and I agreed to meet him there. I didn't bother bringing Danill with me because I trusted the Steele family. They pose no threat to me, and I know it.

I pulled up to the location a few minutes ago, and Jordan was already there. The two of us are now making idle chit-chat when his niece, Leona, shows up. Now, we are just waiting for Emmett.

The shooting area is about forty feet long, possibly twenty feet wide. It's open on each side to all the elements, with only a roof offering protection from the rain or the blazing sun. Booths line the inside, like an actual shooting range. Each person can shoot safely from their booth. I'm speaking with Jordan when I notice a car pulling up on the side. There's already one vehicle here, which belongs to Jordan's lovely niece, Leona.

I realize as he steps out of the car that it's Jordan's nephew, Emmett, and I pay particular attention to him shaking his head in annoyance. He buttons his suit jacket as he approaches his uncle and his sister. "I apologize for the delay. The traffic was a bit of a problem," Emmett says to the group of us.

Jordan waves his hand in dismissal. "It's no problem. Leona and I have it handled."

Emmett's eyes lock with Leona's, and she smiles brightly. "Don't worry. We've hardly started."

"Apologies aren't needed. We understand you're a busy man," Emmett tells me, and I nod in thanks.

"I like this family dynamic you have. Your uncle was telling me this is your younger sister. I hope one day my sister takes the world by the balls like yours does. It's a rarity to have such a strong woman in your family. A blessing, in fact," I comment as I stare at his sister. Though, it's not in a sexual manner. It's a cultural difference. We do things much differently in other parts of the world. Most women are only used to secure alliances, but my hope is that eventually, I can bring Eset into something. She isn't technically an Umarova, but she is my sister, and I will always take care of my family. Nazyr, too, if he wants the opportunity.

Leona giggles in a carefree manner. "Oh goodness, you haven't met my mother. She's the strongest woman I know. She taught me everything about being the woman I am."

I offer the woman a soft smile. "I imagine she must be ferocious."

"Yes, you have no idea," Jordan interrupts, walking over to me and placing a hand behind my shoulder. "I'd love to test your products or taste them, as we should say." We're in public, so we're operating under the guise I'm selling the Steele family liquor. I'd assume we'd be safe to speak freely this far out, but we can never be too sure, I guess.

"Of course, please come," I say, leading them up to the shooting range. Along the back of the building, there are gun cases. We all walk up to them, and Leona heads to the smaller one, pulling out a 9mm Glock.

She walks over to one of the booths and puts on her eye and ear protection. While she's putting ammunition in, the rest of us are putting on our eye and ear protection. Meanwhile, Leona's quick to chamber a round. She tests the 9mm, and it sounds exactly as it should. She continues shooting until she's out, places the gun down, and slides down her earmuffs. "It's good," she looks to her uncle.

He gives a nod, then looks at Emmett. "Emmett, check the AR-10, AR-15, and the AK. Leona, I want you to test the .308, 7mm, and 306. Ruslan and I will look at the rest of his supplies."

Leona and Emmett proceed to do as their uncle says, and I must say they seem impressed with the quality of the guns they're testing. I've seen many men test my product, and they all look the same when they're satisfied. Shocked, but pleasantly so. I'm going to naturally assume this meeting is going as well as possible. In a few short minutes, I should know. If I can get them what they need, it'll help them with their supply shortages.

Within about half an hour, we're all finished testing everything. Emmett's since cleaned the guns he's tested, and Leona's done the same with hers. They then put them back into their proper cases, and I pull Jordan off to the side to speak to him one-on-one. It looks like there might be a bit of sibling rivalry going on, and I don't want it to take away from the business deal.

"It seems to me like you're satisfied, and we can come to an official agreement." I wait to gauge Jordan's reaction, but the man doesn't have one at all. He's stoic, and for a few minutes, I'm almost sweating.

He then extends a hand, and I take it. We shake, and I can rest easy knowing the Steeles are going to move forward with this deal. I didn't think they weren't going to do it, but I know if they had another arm's dealer pop up, I'd be met with some sort of competition. I'm certainly not the only arm's dealer they could work with, but I am the one they want to work with right now. It's a good opportunity for me to prove myself and my position in power. A time to prove to the people who are against me that I can do this, and I am doing it. I know some still remain loyal to Anzor, and acts such as this will make me seem more serious.

"Can you get me a combined mixture of guns on a weekly

shipment? Add a bit of body armor every two weeks, but I don't want to involve myself in the grenades and other miscellaneous items unless there's a specific need. Guns are enough to worry about on the streets. The last thing I need is for someone to toss a grenade and then really shake things up with the ATF."

"I can. Do you want me to include a bit of everything on the first shipment? That way, you have whatever you need if the situation arises?"

Jordan takes a few moments and then nods. "Yes, and if I require more of them, I'll notify you."

"Perfect. I'll make sure to call my people and get everything set up. I take it you have a specific day and shipyard you want me to transport the items to?"

Almost every client, who buys as much as the Steeles are going to, has paid off people. They have whomever they need in their pockets to ensure they won't get busted. "Yes. I'll send over those details later with the first deposit."

"Sounds perfect." I extend my hand again out of courtesy, and Jordan takes it.

"We'll see you again, I'm sure," Jordan tells me, and I nod.

There's no doubt about it. The Steele family is now my biggest customer.

"I'm sure of it. I've become attached to the area, so I'm going to be in Atlanta for a bit longer. It'll make our business dealings a bit easier to handle, I believe," I inform Jordan, noticing Leona and Emmett are coming closer.

"That it will," Jordan replies.

"Perfect. Well, I must be going. There's another situation that requires my attention. If you have any questions, concerns, or troubles, you know how to get in contact with me," I tell Jordan and then head back to my SUV, where I have one of my other guards in the passenger seat. I knew I wouldn't need him out here with me since things with the Steeles are settled, but when I really got down and thought about things, I knew I should at least have one other person here with me.

Now, I wouldn't ever say the Steeles would go against me, but what would happen if they did? It would be just like the situation with Artos at the gas station. Nal is the guard I brought with me today. He typically stays in Grozny, but when he heard I was heading back to Atlanta, he asked if I wanted him to come.

He couldn't leave that day because he has a wife and kids at home, so he flew out late yesterday and arrived first thing this morning. Since he's leaving his wife and kids at home, I've opted to pay him a bit more than his usual salary. Danill makes the highest of all my men, but now Nal is making the second highest. I figure when you leave the ones you love the most behind, you need to be compensated for it.

Nal drives off, and we head for the hotel. We don't even hit the interstate before I get a call. I figure it could be the Steeles wanting to change something about their shipment, so I move quickly while fetching it from my pocket. Only when the caller ID comes across, it's my brother.

"Lom, I wasn't expecting to hear from you."

"Yes, well, I thought you'd want to know we have some dogs out for blood. Anyone who's truly loyal to the Umarova family is heading for Boston. Every one of them wants to see Anzor suffer for what he put you through, and they want him out of the picture. You're their leader, not him."

"What do you mean by dogs? Allies? Chechen people?"

"Chechen people, my brother. It seems we aren't the only ones not pleased with the way Anzor's led. In the last twenty years, crime rates have gone up exponentially. Our father kept crime out of Grozny, and if there were issues, he'd make sure they were hush-hush. Anzor didn't care about upsetting the people of Chechnya. All he ever cared about was money."

I'm not displeased. Chechnya has seen the cruelties that were dealt to my family at Anzor's hand. Many probably saw he was taking advantage of a situation he shouldn't have ever been involved in. If anyone was going to speak for me, it should've been my mother... but our country hasn't taken too keenly to women being in power. Anzor had no place doing everything he's done over the years.

"Have you made any contact with the O'Deas?" The O'Deas are one of the foremost Irish families. Though they're not at the top of the food chain, they work under their cousins, the Mackenzies. They do, however, run everything that happens in Boston, and we'd be fools to head there without speaking to them.

"No, I haven't. I figured you'd be the one to contact Cian," Cian, the eldest son of the O'Dea family, has been the leader for well over twenty years.

"No, I'm going to ask you to do this for me. I have something I need to handle here, so please contact Cian and get whatever authorization you need to." Truth be told, I've been stressed out lately. All of this with Anzor, Artos, and then the bullshit with Amelia's ex-boyfriend, Carter. Ever since the day at the park, I've had a bad feeling about Carter, and then when Danill told me what happened at the club, I knew the man would be trouble.

"All right. I'll do what's needed to be done. Is there anything specific you want me to do when I contact Cian or when I'm in Boston?" I think about it for a few moments, and when it comes to Cian, I don't have anything specific.

"Whenever you have Anzor in your grasp, make sure to bring him here to Atlanta. Nothing is to be done to him in Boston, and he's not to be killed."

"Is your plan to take him back to Chechnya?" Lom questions, and he must think I'm going to be decent to Anzor.

"No. I won't be giving him the dignity of dying in his homeland. He doesn't deserve such a privilege." I might sound cold because he is my stepfather and the father to my two half-siblings, but he's gone against me in ways I will never be able to forgive him for. Anzor may have been around for a large part of my life, but he isn't my family. He's my enemy.

Nal drives me back to the hotel, and he heads into the parking garage. We get out of the vehicle, head for the elevators, and head inside. Within a few minutes, we're up and walking into the suite I've rented here. Though, as I head into the suite, I notice Amelia's curled up on the couch with a blanket, seeming a bit worse for wear.

Danill's sitting about ten feet away from her at the desk in the living room. He's on a laptop, and once he sees I'm back, he motions with his head for me to go to Amelia.

"*Malen'kiy krolik*, what's going on? You seem a bit different."

Amelia swallows hard and grabs the hot cup of tea sitting on the coffee table in front of her. She wraps her hands around the warm mug and looks at me as if she's debating telling me what's wrong.

"You should tell him, Miss Amelia," Danill speaks up.

Amelia shoots her head back around to glare at Danill. "Why? Because you already threatened to if I didn't? I don't need you to act as a guillotine over my head, Danill. I'm an adult, and I'll speak to Ruslan about what I want to, not because I'm being forced to by one of his men." Amelia's tone is laced with venom, and it's evident to me she's furious at Danill. It seems to me he made a mistake in pissing her off. But I want to know what's happened because something obviously has.

Danill turns his head and realizes Nal is with me. "Nal, it is good to see you."

"Likewise," Nal says to Danill.

Amelia looks past me and at Nal. "I'm not normally so bitchy, so I apologize. It's great to meet you."

Nal smirks at Amelia's words. "Likewise. I've heard very good things about you, Miss Amelia." Nal walks over to where Danill is and takes a seat beside him.

Meanwhile, I take a seat next to Amelia and wrap my arm around her. "Are you going to tell me what's going on?"

Amelia runs a hand through her hair and sighs heavily. "I wanted to get out of the suite for a bit, so I went for a walk," Amelia pauses, and I somewhat glare at her. She's forgetting one important piece of information here. "Don't worry, I didn't go alone. Danill was a little ways behind me the entire time. So I had my earphones in and was walking, taking in the scenery and all that. I rounded the corner and ran straight into Carter. When I mean I ran into him, I mean I *literally* ran into him."

I glance at Danill, and he doesn't seem pleased in the least bit. He knows as much as I do that there's something fishy going on here. "What did he say to you?"

"He said, and I quote, 'I knew I'd run into you again, Amelia.'" Amelia closes her eyes as she speaks. I can tell this has shaken her up a bit, and I understand why. From what I know about her previous relationship, he was cruel to her. She dealt with what she could, but she ignored a lot of the red flags at the time. I think being with me now has shown her what she should look for in a man and what isn't appropriate.

"What did you do?" I ask her, and I run my hand along her shoulder. I'm trying to reassure her, to silently tell her I'm here for her and that she's okay.

"I didn't have to do anything. Danill came up right behind me and pushed Carter out of the way." Amelia takes a sip of the tea and then swallows before speaking again. "He said he looked forward to seeing me later and then tomorrow. He said I looked pretty in the dress I wore to meet with Emily the other day. It… it made me sick to my stomach, Ruslan." The more she speaks, the angrier I get. "I thought he was the one at the club, and I knew I felt eyes on me. I didn't have any idea he was following me to meet with Emily too."

I stop rubbing her arm and hold her against me. "I'm going to handle this, Amelia. You don't have to worry anymore about it. Okay?"

Amelia turns her head to stare into my eyes. "I'm afraid to ask what you're going to do."

"You don't have to ask, but if you want to know, I'll tell you."

She nods once, and I'm going to tell her something, but it won't be in-depth. "I'll make sure he doesn't bother you ever again." I don't plan on killing Carter, but if he pisses me off enough, I just might.

"Okay," Amelia sighs, and I know she's really bothered by him following her around.

"I tell you what. I'll fix you a bath with some of those oils you bought in Grozny. You can take a long, hot bath, drink some wine, and read a book. I'll have Danill order you whatever you want for dinner, and then I'll be back later tonight. We can watch some movies or something if you're still home. How does that sound?"

"Sure," Amelia mutters, and I know what I'm saying doesn't make up for how she feels. Though, once I do what needs to be done, I'm sure she'll feel a lot better.

I press a kiss to her forehead and rise from the couch, head for the bathroom, and turn on the bath. I make sure it's very hot; this way, she can get in whenever she wants to. I grab one of the oils she got in Grozny. It's called Lavender Rose Water, so I put a few drops in the tub, just as the directions state. There are a few tea-light candles around the tub, so I put those on and head back out to the living area.

Nal and Danill are both behind the laptop, and I notice from the corner of my eye what program they're looking at. It's one used to gain access to people's private information like physical addresses and phone numbers. If we can't find an accurate address for him, we should be able to ping his phone and narrow it down to a couple of blocks. From that point, all we have to do is make a connection and see if he has friends or family in the area where his phone is pinging.

Amelia heads off to the bathroom and shuts the bedroom door behind her. I walk over to where Nal and Danill are, and Danill looks at me. "His cell's been pinging at this one tower for over a week, and our software has traced his GPS location to this house."

"We were able to track down exactly where he was with this?" There must've been some updates over the last few weeks. Before, it took us a bit longer to get everything we needed.

"Yes. He has his GPS on, so it was very easy to track him down," Nal chimes in. I've never been more grateful for the way phones have advanced over the years.

"Perfect. I'm heading over there now. Danill, stay with Amelia. Nal, come with me for backup." Nal rises from his seat, and the two of us head out. Neither of us speaks during the elevator ride or even when we get into the SUV. We're quiet for most of the way, except when we're rounding the corner to where the house Carter's staying at is.

I have Nal park the car around the corner from where Carter's phone has been pinging. We walk outside and approach the home. It's in a rougher part of Atlanta, and a couple of the windows at the top are boarded up, but there are lights on inside. Nal goes to one side of the house while I take the other. I want to take Carter by surprise, so I push open the back gate and walk down the overgrown cement path.

Sure enough, Carter's out back at a fire pit. He has a beer in his hand and hasn't heard a thing. I knock the beer out of his hand and pull out my knife, wrapping my arm around his neck and pressing the blade against his neck.

"Right about now is when you start to wonder what I'm here for. You're debating if something in front of you could be used as a tool to take me out, but you won't find anything. Nothing can help you, Carter, because you've angered the wrong man. I could cut your throat right now and let it be the end of everything, but I think you're a coward who will learn. Are you someone who learns, Carter, or are you a man who will repeat his mistakes?"

Carter jolts against my grip and tries to wriggle free.

"Fighting won't help you. I don't think I need to say it again. Answer me. What are you?"

"I learn. Yep. I learn," Carter says, emotion flooding his voice. It's obvious he's worried about getting out of here alive.

"This is when you ask, what can I do better." I press the knife further against his neck, knowing the blade is piercing him.

"W-what can I do better?" His words come out staggered, and he truly fears for his life right now.

"You leave Amelia alone. That's what you can do better. You don't go near her, and if you're ever within a mile of her again, I'll make sure you can never take another breath." Just as I finish speaking, Nal comes around the other side of the house and approaches us. Carter can't see him because of the angle, and I motion with my head for Nal to come closer.

Nal gets within a couple feet of Carter and me, and then Nal grabs Carter by the back of the shirt. He shoves him into the fire and holds him there for a good few seconds, his face directly on top of the flame. Carter screams bloody murder, but that won't stop us. Nal yanks him off the fire and pulls him back, holding him for me.

I ball my hand into a fist and repeatedly slam it into his face. Blood begins coming out at me with every punch, and Carter continues to scream. He keeps screaming with every punch, but it won't do anything. I'm going to leave him here scarred, bloody, and beaten. That's what he gets for terrifying her so badly, and if he keeps it up, he'll be dead.

Chapter Thirteen

Amelia

Ruslan told me to take a nice relaxing bath, and I did. I sat in the tub for well over an hour, letting the oils soak into my body. The bathroom smelled of a mixture between lavender and roses. It was very subtle, and I think it was exactly what I needed to feel better. Sometimes, all you need is a little self-care.

Earlier today, running into Carter scared me half to death. It was traumatic enough dealing with him when we were together, and then all of a sudden, I started seeing him pop up in other places. I thought I'd finally gotten rid of him when he left. I showed up, and all his things were gone. I could tell he left in a hurry, but I didn't know why. As the days went on, I began to understand why—because he's guilty. It's what I think, at least.

Deep in my gut, I know he had something to do with the money that went missing at Illusion, and I'm beginning to think he could've had a hand to play in my identity theft too. I didn't see it before, but being with Ruslan has opened my eyes in a lot of ways. I understand a lot more about what people will do for themselves. Now, I don't want to go and think everyone's selfish and greed-fueled, but a lot of people are, and I'm not blind to it.

Ruslan said he'd come back home, and then we could watch some movies. He even told Danill to let me order whatever I wanted. I didn't want anything too crazy, so I ordered some steamed pork dumplings. In my eyes, there isn't anything better. It's heavy comfort food for any time of day, hot or cold. Then again, Chinese food is one of my absolute favorites. I already ate, drank a bottle of water, and even blow-dried my hair.

I've been sitting on the couch, and a little while ago, I grew tired, so I grabbed the blanket I was holding onto when Ruslan came home earlier and laid down. For a hotel couch, this one is very nice and comfortable. It isn't too firm, but it isn't too soft, either. It's the perfect mixture of the two, honestly. It wasn't hard for me to doze off. I don't know how long I was asleep, but the scuffing of feet awakens me.

I blink a few times and look around, seeing Nal and Ruslan have come back. Ruslan's suit is a bit disheveled. His forehead is lined with sweat, and I notice a red mark on his dress shirt that wasn't there before.

"Are you okay? What happened?" I immediately question as I stand up and walk over to him.

"Nothing I couldn't handle," Ruslan tells me and then looks over to Danill. A moment later, Danill is leaving with Nal, and it's just the two of us left in the suite.

"You have to give me more than that. Where did you go off to? What did you do? I thought I'd come out of the bathroom, and you'd be back already… but it's been three hours, Ruslan. I fell asleep on the couch." I'm not overly angered with him, but I'm annoyed. I was scared to death earlier, and he left me here with Danill. What I wanted was for him to be here with me, to hold me, kiss me, and comfort me. I don't think it's too much to ask for, not in the least bit.

"I handled it as quickly as I could," Ruslan states, but obviously, he was out doing something else. What takes three hours to handle?

"I can't deal with your vagueness right now," I grit, glaring at him with all my might.

"I don't owe you any answers, Amelia. I don't owe you shit. You can question me all you want about what I did, but it doesn't mean I'm going to answer you." He has no idea what sort of hole he's just dug for himself. I had some sort of idea that he'd try to track down Carter and knock some sense into him, but was he doing something else? Is that why it looks like there's blood on his dress shirt?

His speaking to me this way pisses me off so much. Who the fuck does he think he is? I've never spoken to him like this because I actually respect him.

"You've got to be fucking kidding me right now." I can't hold back my rage one bit. I thought about it for a second, but I have to get this out. I have to get this awful feeling out of my chest before I combust under all this pressure. "You have some balls speaking to me like I don't matter to you when we both know it isn't true in the least. It's belittling, and I don't deserve it at all. I've had too many relationships where I was belittled or made to feel awful, and I'm not going to do it again. I'm not fucking doing it! You've taught me what I deserve and how to stick up for myself, so here I am doing it. I'm not going to do this, Ruslan. I refuse to be spoken to like I'm a piece of shit. If you're going to keep talking to me like this, I'm going to leave, and I won't ever look back. Not once. That's what you'll get for your actions, me disappearing like I'm in a fucking magic show. So stop talking to me like I'm shit on the bottom of your shoe." I shake my head, and tears begin to fill my eyes.

Ruslan was cruel to me the first day I met him because he had to be. Because he was working to help the Steeles find their missing money, but he stuck his neck out to keep me safe and paid back my debt. I was certain he wouldn't be cruel to me beyond that, but here he is, proving me wrong. He's proving that he can be foul whenever he wants to be.

Out of nowhere, Ruslan grabs me by my throat and looks into my eyes. There isn't an ounce of regret in his action, either. He licks his lips and very calmly speaks up. "You don't have a fucking choice in the matter,

Amelia. You never did. I bought your life, remember? I'm the only reason you're still breathing right now." Every single word sounds laced with fury, and I don't understand it.

Before he left the suite earlier, he seemed so dedicated to defending me… and now his anger's directed toward me? It doesn't make sense.

Ruslan tightens his grip around my throat and backs me against the couch. I plop down onto the cushion, and he unbuttons and then unzips his pants, revealing his already hard cock. Jesus. Was he turned on when he came home, or did my tongue turn him on?

"It looks like I need to give your tongue something else to focus on," he tells me and pulls my neck toward his cock.

I debate biting it off, but I really love our sex life. I open my mouth and take his cock in my mouth. I go back and forth, swirling my tongue around his head with every movement. He lightly moans, so I tug at his pants to bring them down. I palm his balls with one hand while sucking on his dick. I notice, over time, that when I apply pressure on his balls and suck hard, he goes apeshit. He moans in pleasure, and my own body heats up every time I hear his pleasure.

Ruslan drives his fingers into my hair and holds on tight, then pushes me to increase speed. I open wider for him, and my mouth is so wet. "Fuck, yes. Keep it up, *malen'kiy krolik*." His voice comes out gravelly, and I know he's getting closer. I don't want him to come yet, though. I want more than just a quick blowjob.

He begins thrusting his hips and shoves his dick so far down my throat that I start to gag. I don't know why, but I think it's so fucking hot. Ruslan pulls his cock out of my mouth and scoops me into his arms like I weigh nothing. He carries me down the hall until we reach the bedroom, and he shuts the door with his foot.

Ruslan tosses me on the bed and gives me one stern look. "Strip, now."

I almost want to ask him if he remembers how he spoke to me… but

I really want to get laid too. Ruslan is the best lover I've ever had, and maybe if he gets his shit together, he'll continue to be.

I remove the cozy pajama shirt and the shorts I've been wearing since I took my bath. I hardly ever wear underwear, just because I'm not a big fan of them. I'm left here on our cream-colored sheets, naked and willing.

Ruslan begins taking his own clothes off. First, it's his suit jacket, then his dress shirt, and the undershirt below it. He kicks off his shoes and then takes off his pants and boxers too. They were simply hanging at his knees when we were out in the living room. "Lay your head over the edge of the bed." He instructs, and I follow his directions like a good girl.

God, what's become of me? What happened to the woman who was telling him what she would and wouldn't do? I suppose none of it matters now that I'm distracted with Ruslan. It makes me feel pathetic but having sex with him makes me feel powerful. I've never felt that way before, but I'm here fully embracing this divine femininity.

Ruslan lines his cock up with my mouth and forces himself deep down my throat. I sense heat around my clit, and Ruslan lowers his lips over it. Electricity rushes through me when his lips close around it, and I roll my head back a bit more while he thrusts his cock down my throat. I breathe in and out through my nose and moan around it when he starts teasing me.

He brings his fingers against my lips and rubs them delicately. He twirls and spins while doing the same with his tongue. I roll my hips against his mouth, and he increases his own thrusting. I can't believe I've been with any other person before him. They never made my body scream the way he does. They've never even tried. It makes me wish I had met Ruslan years ago, and he was my first because I know he would've taken care of me. He would always make sure I was okay in general, but sexually, he'd make sure I felt powerful like I do right now.

Heat centers around my lower region, and I don't think I'm about to come yet, but I keep getting wetter by the moment. He makes slurping sounds with his mouth as he sucks on my clit and even begins to flick it with his tongue. It sends my body into overdrive, but I don't want to be mouth fucked right now. I want his dick in me.

I press against his hips in an attempt to push him away, but he grabs my hands and forces them down. Ruslan fucks my mouth harder than he's ever fucked my pussy, and my eyes water from how much he's hitting my gag reflex.

Out of nowhere, he pulls his cock out of me and flips me around like I'm a ragdoll. He has me in doggy-style position and, without warning, shoves his cock deep inside me. I scream from the sudden intrusion, and Ruslan grabs me by the throat once more. "No one has the right to tell me what I'm going to do. Not even you."

Chapter Fourteen

Ruslan

I shouldn't have treated her so horribly last night. It was the first thing I thought about this morning when I woke up. I'd been cruel to her, and she knows it. All she's ever known is men being cruel to her, and I showed Amelia I wasn't any different. Even now, I'm shaking my head at my stupidity. She's a diamond in the rough, and yet I've done something that could completely fuck everything up.

When I woke up this morning, Amelia wasn't there. I was worried she'd flown the coop but was relieved when Danill wasn't in the suite either. At least she was smart enough to take him with her, even if she was angry at me. I've heard from friends in my life that when our wives or girlfriends are mad at us, it can be the worst. Out of spite, they'll sometimes run from us and ditch their security detail. Hopefully, it's something I can speak to Amelia about, and afterward, she won't do it. That's the hope, anyway.

First thing this morning, I ordered ten dozen red roses to be delivered by six in the evening today. It's a bit past ten in the evening now. Amelia's working at Illusion tonight, so she should come home and be blown away by everything I'm organizing for her. I'm going to have candles lit, roses everywhere, her favorite foods, and sparkling wine.

I haven't spoken to Lom in a couple of days since he said he was going to Boston, but I imagine he's doing everything he can to find Anzor. I'm not the only one who's angered with Anzor's decisions. Lom wasn't on board in the beginning because I think he felt as though I was attacking our mother. In a way, I was, yes, but I wasn't blaming her for her husband's actions. Do I feel like she could've stood up for what she believed in more? Yes, I do. But I'm forced to remember the time. Only very recently did women in criminal organizations begin speaking up.

Within the last twenty years, a woman took over the Russian Bratva, and a woman took over the Romanian Clans. As far as the Clans go, it isn't so new. Mariana Petran was the only daughter of the Petran family, who'd been head of the Romanian organization for many, many years. Her eldest child happened to be a daughter, and Mariana made it so that Bianca could rightfully be the one in charge. Bianca was a child conceived in rape, and Mariana ended up marrying Ion Petran after she was rescued from her captor. The captor fathered her child, but Ion didn't care about it. He raised that little girl, and if anyone asked him when he was alive, Ion would say Bianca was his. He would've shot down anyone who deemed otherwise as well.

When it comes to my mother, I think there will always be a small part of me that's upset with her. I don't mean to hold onto that anger, but it's not so simple to let it go.

I'm sitting on the couch in the living room, texting with Eset, when my phone begins to ring. It's the identity theft firm I hired a couple weeks ago to look into Amelia's case. I immediately tap the green button and bring the phone to my ear. "Hello."

"Hello. Is this Ruslan?"

"Yes, it is," I tell the woman on the other side of the phone.

"Hi Ruslan, this is Maggie from Identity Theft Alliance. How are you doing today?" It might be late, but I gave the firm explicit instructions to contact me as soon as they could with any sort of updates. The time of day didn't matter. I wanted answers as soon as they became available.

"I'm doing all right. Thank you. How about yourself?" I don't want to waste time with idle chit-chat, but I know the sooner I get this over with, the sooner I'll have an update on Amelia's case.

"I'm just dandy, thank you for asking. So the reason I'm calling is that we've made an update on your case for Amelia. It's very rare that we get something so quickly, and I figured you'd be pleased to get the update."

"Yes, I am. What's the update? I'm a bit eager to hear about it."

"Yes, of course. So there are many factors we look into when it comes to identity theft cases. You specifically requested we do everything we could to try and track down these criminals, and that's what we've done for you here, Ruslan. Now, the biggest break, in this case, is also a bit concerning, so I need to make you aware of that. You gave us an address for Amelia, and I want to verify that with you."

"Okay."

Maggie proceeds to verify Amelia's address for her apartment, and I'm not sure why she's even verifying it with me, to be honest. I've already done this.

She sighs on the other end but clears her throat. "We traced the IP address back to the address where Amelia resides. Now, that's not to say she's the one responsible for it. Does she have any roommates, parents, exes, or anything of that sort? They would've had to have been there within the last year."

Emily just moved in with Amelia not too long ago, and before Amelia, there was only one other person—Carter.

I hate this for Amelia, but it's nice to finally get confirmation. I suspected he had something to do with her identity theft. Deep in my bones, I knew he was trouble, and I was right. "What does this mean for the case?"

"It means we've gone pretty far. The only other thing we can do is figure out the owner of that computer. Right now, we have the IP address, which is helpful… but do you have any idea who was living with Amelia at the time of her identity theft?"

"I'm not aware of who was living with her at that time. I'll have to check with her and get back to you guys." I lie to this woman because I don't want there to be any recording that could incriminate me. Yes, we know exactly who's responsible for this. I'll be damned if I give anyone else the pleasure of dealing with him except me. Amelia is my woman, and this is my responsibility. Not to mention my privilege.

"Certainly! Just give me a call on this line when you have that information for me. Okay?" Maggie tells me, and I agree before we say a quick goodbye.

As soon as the call ends with Maggie, I call up Nal. He was with me last night at the house Carter's renting. Within a few moments, he answers. "Boss, what's up?"

"I got an update on Amelia's identity theft case. I need you and Danill on board to help. Carter's responsible for it all. An IP address was tracked back to Amelia's apartment, and I know she didn't steal her own identity."

"Fuck, that's intense. Want me to call Danill and notify him?" Nal asks.

"Yes, actually. I need to make a call to Amelia's boss in the meantime. Go back to Carter's house. We'll be lucky if he hasn't packed up his shit and run. If I had confirmation that he did this last night, I wouldn't have ever let him go."

"Yes, sir. I'll get in contact with Danill and head straight there."

"Good, but do not go on that property alone, Nal. I'm living proof of what happens to people when they go in without at least one other person." I've learned so much from the gas station. The last thing I want to do is put my men in a similar situation.

"Understood. I'll call or text you with an update when I have one," Nal says as he ends the phone call.

I call Illusion, and a woman answers. I tell her I need to speak to Gregor, and within a few moments, I have him on the phone. I tell him who I am, and he recognizes my voice. I don't give him too much information, but I ask him to keep an eye on Amelia until the end of her shift because Danill will be stepping away to handle something.

Gregor tells me the club's been unusually slow tonight and that he was going to cut a couple of the women early. He says he'll cut Amelia early, and I tell him that I'll be there in twenty minutes to pick her up. This way, I don't have to worry about her being at the club at all. I can simply go there, get her in the car and bring her home. Maybe then I can properly make up for how I treated her last night and give her the same update I received tonight.

I wait a few minutes and then head over to Illusion. When I get there, she's surprised to see me, but I don't think it's a bad surprise. Amelia gets in the passenger side of the SUV. We don't talk too much, but once we get back to the parking garage of the hotel, she finally begins to speak.

"Are you going to tell me why Danill left and you picked me up? Gregor was cutting people since it was slow, so I don't think you had anything to do with that."

I walk up to her and take her hand in mine, giving it a slight squeeze. "Yeah. I needed Danill to go with Nal to handle something. I picked you up since Danill wasn't with you, and I wanted to see you. I feel terrible for how I spoke to you, Amelia. You were right. You don't deserve to be spoken to like that. I was angry, and I took my anger out on you, which isn't acceptable. I only hope you can forgive me for it."

Amelia smiles softly. "You know, after the sixth orgasm last night, I think I forgave you. But it's nice to hear you actually say you're sorry. I wanted to talk to you about it, so I'm glad you brought it up."

I stop in my tracks and pull Amelia against me. All I want is to have my arms around her and know she's safe. I kiss the top of her head and tug her hand along with me. "Come, I have a surprise for you."

Amelia and I get into the elevator, and within a few minutes, the doors open to our suite. Her breath's taken away when she steps foot into the room. It looks straight out of a hotel ad for a romantic weekend getaway. Roses, candles, chilled sparkling wine. I'd do anything for this woman. I'd burn down the entire world if she asked me to. Though, sometimes I wonder if she realizes how savage I'd become for her.

"Ruslan, this is beautiful."

"Not as beautiful as you, *malen'kiy krolik*. I do have another present for you."

Amelia raises both of her brows. "Oh? What kind of present?"

"The firm I hired to look into your identity theft called me this evening. They found the location of the person who was behind it all."

Amelia's eyes go wide. "What? Really? Where?" She seems almost excited to hear this.

"Yes. Your apartment," as soon as I tell her it was her own place, her excited expression shifts to shock and fear.

"That means Carter did this." Amelia swallows and runs as fast as she can to the closest bathroom. It's right off the living room, and she drops to her knees. In no time, she's vomiting in the toilet, and I'm grabbing her hair and holding it, so she doesn't get any vomit in it.

"We got him, Amelia. This is good. We know it was him." I try to reassure her, but I have no idea what sort of things are running through her mind right now.

I hand Amelia a washcloth, and she wipes her mouth. She looks at me with disgust in her eyes, and as soon as she speaks, I feel so sorry for her. "I trusted him, and he violated me in the most horrific of ways."

Chapter Fifteen

Amelia

I'm leaning over the porcelain throne, trying to keep myself from throwing up any more than I already have. My head pounds, and my stomach's rolling in the worst way possible.

Carter's responsible for my identity theft.

I know Ruslan didn't lie to me. He would never lie to me about something like this. Still, my mouth's fallen open, and I'm completely perplexed. But why shouldn't I be? Carter took advantage of me, sure. I think I knew it back when I was dating him, but I didn't have any clue just how much he was doing it. He's solely responsible for all the hell I've been through the last year. I even vented to him, cried in front of him, and screamed at the world when I was with him. All those emotionally charged, frustrating outbursts where I kept asking why it was happening to me, and he told me people target others. He said it just happened, and it happened to millions of people, but he said over time, everything would be okay again. He was probably laughing at me when I walked away, smiling because he was the man responsible for it all.

God, it makes me so sick. Another bout of nausea comes coursing through me, and I don't know what I'm going to do. Ruslan's sitting on the bathroom floor next to me, still holding my hair. "I'm sorry to tell you this way, but I knew you'd want to know what happened."

I give him a curt nod but shake my head in disbelief. How could I not have noticed? How could I not have realized he was the one behind it all? I feel so idiotic. The man had access to all my private information. He knew where my lock box was with my birth certificate, social security card, and passport. I even have all my bank information in that lockbox. Whatever he needed to get, he could. He could've picked the lock on the box for all I know, or maybe he even had an extra key made. There are so many things running through my mind right now, things I should've paid more attention to when I was with him.

"Stop that," Ruslan speaks out of nowhere, and I look into his dark eyes.

"Stop what, Ruslan?" I ask him, my exhaustion and stress showing in my voice.

"Overthinking. I see it on your face. You're blaming yourself right now, aren't you?" It never ceases to amaze me how Ruslan knows exactly what I'm thinking. Not all of the time, but there's a good portion where it's like he has a mind-reading device.

"How can't I? I let him into my apartment. I let him into my life... and look what he did, Ruslan. He fucked it all up. He's the reason I've been so stressed. I don't expect you to understand it because you have money. You could make this go away with the snap of your fingers, but I can't. I'm not well off like you are. I'm a regular woman who's busting my ass to try and get this all sorted. Identity theft isn't something that'll just come right off your credit. It takes a while, and if I'm lucky, it might be expunged from my credit within the next couple of years. No one will let me get a credit card, open a bank account, or even apply for a loan. If anyone does a background check on me, I won't get approved for an apartment, job, or whatever it is. That's how badly identity theft screws you."

Ruslan lets go of my hair and gently rubs my back. I know he's trying to think of what he can say to make me feel better, but he's not going to be able to make me feel better. This is my life, as pathetic and fucked up as it is right now. If it weren't for him, I might never have found out Carter did this.

Tears well in my eyes and slowly cascade down my cheeks. As much as I try, I can't hold them back. I'm both sad at finding this out and grateful for Ruslan being in my life. He might not have come in under the best circumstances, but he's already making such a positive impact on my life.

"You aren't in this alone. We found out who did it, and I'm going to make him pay. I will do that for you." Ruslan stares into my eyes, and I know he's trying to reassure me.

I let out a soft laugh and keep eye contact with him. "You'd do anything for me, Ruslan, and I know it."

Ruslan wraps his arm around me and pulls me into his lap. He presses a chaste kiss on the top of my head. "You have no idea how important you are to me, do you?" Ruslan's question comes out of nowhere.

I glance up at him, and he simply stares into my eyes, but the air is different now. It isn't thick, but it isn't as still as it was a few moments ago. Suddenly, heat comes over me, and I'm rendered speechless.

"To me, you are the sun that rises in the morning and sets in the night. My world starts and ends with you, Amelia. When I met you that night at Illusion, when I thought you took the money, I had no idea our lives would lead to this moment. I simply thought you were a woman who was a bold-faced thief or at least an accomplice. Though, now I know you're neither. You're a woman who was treated poorly for far too long. You're a survivalist, and in no way are you a victim. That word doesn't suit you. I know sometimes you think you're a victim, but I'm here to tell you that you are not. I… I'm having a bit of difficulty finding the words I want to convey to you right now."

I wrap my arm around Ruslan and wait for him to say something more, not wanting to interrupt this moment.

"I never thought I'd want you in the way I crave. I never thought I'd stick my neck out for you and put my reputation on the line, but alas, I did it because I knew you were in danger if I didn't. On that day, I knew I wanted you in my life, and on this day, I know I don't want you to ever not be in my life. I want you by my side until the end of days." Ruslan stops speaking abruptly, and I start to get a bit nervous. Is this some sort of proposal?

"We haven't labeled this relationship between us, but I do think we've considered each other as partners for some time. I want to make that known, Amelia. You are mine as I am yours. I walked into this with you as an arrangement to pay back the money that was stolen, but that isn't what this is. The money I paid to get you out of trouble means nothing to me. You, on the other hand, mean everything."

I release a pent-up breath and pull Ruslan against me. I don't kiss him because I threw up a few minutes ago, and I'm not trying to be disgusting. Moments like these make me realize I could very well fall in love with Ruslan if I'm not in love with him already.

"Come, let's get you some anti-nausea medication. Then we can see if your stomach is settled enough to eat." Ruslan says as he rises, taking me up with him. He's come a long way since the day he came back to me. His strength is coming back, and he's putting on weight. He looks amazing.

Ruslan and I head into the rest of the suite, and I almost forgot how beautiful it looks. Roses, candles, and what looks to be sparkling wine are out. There are even metal food covers over two dishes. He really prepared something special for us tonight, and I don't ever want that to stop. He's an absolute delight, even when he's being a total asshole, but I wouldn't trade it for the world.

Ruslan gives me some anti-nausea medicine even though I tell him I'm fine. I know the shock of finding out Carter was behind it all threw me for a loop, upsetting my stomach in the process. I end up taking the medication to appease Ruslan as I figure it can't hurt. After I take it, I brush my teeth, and the two of us sit down on the couch and talk.

A short time later, we end up eating dinner. He ordered lobster tails, steak, and shrimp scampi for the both of us, with a medley of vegetables. He opened the sparkling wine, and now we are sipping it while out on the balcony. His suite is lovely on the inside, but the outside is amazing too.

The balcony has what looks to be wood floors, but I'm not sure it's actually wood. I assume it isn't because the rain would surely ruin it, so it must be some other material made to look like wood. On the balcony are a few chairs with plush cushions. They're the ones you can lean back on and sunbathe if the mood strikes you. On the sides and in the front of the balcony are potted shrubs that have been perfectly landscaped. They must have someone come up here and trim them quite often.

If we stand, we can get a beautiful view of the city, but the shrubbery gives us a sense of privacy which is very nice. My phone pings, and I glance over to the table beside us, immediately furrowing my brows when I see who it is.

From: Mom

Amelia, we need to talk soon.

I huff as I read the message and put my phone back down where it was.

Ruslan cranes his neck to look at me. "What's stressing you out? I see it all over your face."

I wave my hand in dismissal. "Nothing, really. Just my mother."

"Ignore her for the night. You've already dealt with enough today." Ruslan wraps an arm around me and pulls me on top of him. My legs are planted on either side of his hips, and he snakes a hand up to the side of my face.

He gently caresses me as he brings his lips up to mine for a kiss. I could melt straight into his touch. When I'm with him, nothing else matters. He calms my chaos, and I know he's going to be doing it for years to come.

Ruslan forces his tongue past my lips, and I moan into his mouth, open and willing for whatever he's about to give me. With his other hand, he hikes my skirt over my hips and rubs his fingertips against my bare thigh.

It sends shockwaves over my body, and I find myself grinding against his hips. We pause our kissing for a few moments to take a breath, but it isn't for long. The two of us can't keep our hands off each other. I roll my hips harder and faster against his hips, and his cock comes to life. All I'm doing right now is some pretty intense dry humping, but I love foreplay. It makes the sex that much more incredible when you finally get to it.

"Amelia," Ruslan's plea comes out deep and throaty. All I want to do is pop his cock free from his pants and ride him until the sun comes up. In fact, I might just do it.

I fumble with his button and zipper. He helps me get his cock out, and the moment it's free, I'm stroking my hand against his swollen member. God, he's so hard and ready for me. I want to tease him a bit more, but the more he kisses me, the more I want to feel him sink inside me.

I yank my lips away from his and bite my lip. I want him to watch my face as I slide over his cock, and I do. He hisses with every inch I go down until I'm nestled perfectly on top of him. "Fuck me," Ruslan curses, and a twisted smile covers my lips.

I lean down and press my lips right against his ear. "That's exactly what I plan on doing." He softly moans at my whisper, and I begin to roll my hips against him. He plants one hand on my thigh and keeps another on my side. He slides his hands up every once in a while and palms my breasts as I bounce on his cock.

I suck in a sharp breath when he pushes against my abdomen, forcing me to lean back a bit. With every movement, I feel his cock grinding against my G-spot. It's almost too much, but it's damn near perfect.

My pussy grows wetter by the moment, and I know I won't be able to do this too much longer before I come. I want nothing more than to keep riding him for a few hours before having a massive explosion, but his hand is on my abdomen, and he's forcing me to torture myself. When I say every movement is hypersensitive, I mean it's every damn movement.

"Ruslan." I'm almost begging him to let me move forward, and I try to, but he pushes a bit more firmly on my abdomen.

"No, you ride my cock until your juices are soaking my balls, *malen'kiy krolik*." The moment he says my nickname in that gravelly voice of his, I lose it. I come undone around him. I stop riding him, and Ruslan takes it upon himself to grab onto my hips and fuck me at that angle. My juices come squirting out of me, and I dig my nails into his chest as hard as I can because I'm damn near certain I've never come this hard in my life.

I finish the wave of the orgasm, and Ruslan turns me over on all fours, hikes my skirt up higher, and shoves his cock back into my pussy. "I'm not stopping until this whole balcony smells like the two of us."

I turn my head back and look at Ruslan, staring into his eyes. "Good. I want you to come inside me, please. Fill me up. Fill me up until there isn't any more room," I beg Ruslan, and the man smiles bigger than I've ever seen him before.

Chapter Sixteen

Ruslan

Sunlight beaming in through the windows causes me to wake up. I blink a few times, and our bedroom is as bright as ever. Then I look over to my left, and Amelia's naked body is curled in the sheets. Her brunette hair is sprawled across her pillow, and she has the comforter pulled flush against her chest.

I wrap my arm around Amelia and pull her against me, stirring her awake. She groggily flutters her eyelids, and the second she sees me, she smiles. "Morning, beautiful," I whisper to her and kiss her on the nose before capturing her lips in a kiss.

She wraps her arms around my torso and holds on tight, smiling the longer my lips are on hers. This is what I want our life to be like for the next thirty years. Every day I want it to be like this, where I wake up to her smiling, loving her life with me.

Late last night, I received a text message from my brother, Lom, saying Nazyr and Eset were also in Boston. Apparently, they've been here for a few days to help locate their father. It unnerved me a bit to know Nazyr and Eset are in America, especially when they know the lengths I plan on going to. I'm very well aware Anzor is their father, and I will do something heinous to him whenever I see him face-to-face, but their being here won't cause me to act any differently. Anzor will die at my hand, and nothing will change that.

"Do you want to have breakfast together? I have a busy day planned to deal with work obligations." Amelia immediately raises her brows, and I'm under the impression she knows I must be close to having my stepfather within my grasp.

"Yeah, I'm going out with Emily today. She has the day off, and we thought we'd go shopping or do something fun."

"That's a great idea. Let me treat the two of you to whatever you want."

"Ruslan, you don't need to do that. I have my own money. I can pay for myself," Amelia tells me as she runs her hand along my chest. She holds onto my gold chain at the bottom like she typically does.

"I know you do, but let me spoil you every once in a while. You are my girl, and I enjoy treating you and your cousin to a girl's day out. Danill will be going with you, I take it?"

Amelia rolls her eyes, "Obviously. I haven't jumped my security detail yet."

"Yet is the key factor there. One day, you'll get so angry at me that you think it'll be a smart idea. Let me fill you in on this spoiler. It won't be, so don't act crass with anger and get yourself hurt in the process."

"I'm not going to slip my detail. Danill is great at keeping me safe, and I honestly feel safer with him around, especially with Carter low-key stalking me. Danill's become a good friend to me too." Amelia smiles softly, and I wonder what in the hell Danill and Amelia could be talking about when I'm not around. Would it be better for me to have a woman guarding her?

"Ah, so make sure to include him when you go get manicures and pedicures. Tell him I ordered it, will you?"

Amelia giggles and throws her head back on the pillow. "Oh God, he's going to love that."

"I'm sure he will." I chuckle and roll out of bed. Amelia's right behind me, and we both proceed to get dressed. The two of us head into the bathroom attached to our suite and wash off our faces, comb our hair, and do anything else we need to get done.

We have breakfast in the small kitchen. It's nothing special, but we both have brown sugar oatmeal with fresh raspberries and a cup of coffee each. When Lom texted me last night, he told me to call him, so I did that before I fell asleep. He was already in the process of transporting our stepfather to Georgia, so I could deal with him accordingly. Nazyr and Eset are already with him.

Before I leave the suite, I dig into my wallet and give Amelia one of my cards. I tell her not to go too crazy with it, and she tells me she won't, but I somehow think if the mood strikes, she could do a lot of damage. She might not slip a security detail when she's pissed, but I'd bet she'd rack up my credit card out of spite.

Nal comes with me while Danill stays with Amelia. I sent Lom an address to an old factory in the middle of nowhere. The Steele family owns it, and Jordan is allowing me to use the factory in the meantime. He actually invited me over to an early dinner with him and his family tonight, so I will have to do that. He said he wanted to work together to finalize our business agreement. I thought we were already settled, but there must be something else he needs from me.

Nal and I head for East Atlanta, where the Steeles' old factory is. It's nestled in the countryside and is located on eighty acres, which is perfect for wanting to stay out of the hustle and bustle of the city. It'll give me the opportunity to do whatever I wish to my stepfather as well, without having to worry about prying ears or someone calling the police.

Nal and I finally arrive at the old factory, and there's only one road leading back to it. You can tell it hasn't been paved in years because there are bits of grass and weeds coming up from the blacktop. We continue forward and pass the woods that surround the factory, which add to the seclusion factor. I feel very grateful that Jordan is being so accommodating. It's something I won't forget, and it's something very hard to find. It makes me feel as though our business arrangement is going to be a long-term effort for both of us. I'm hoping so, at least.

I pull the SUV up to an old, rusted building. It's massive in length, probably a few football fields long, and there's graffiti sprayed on the outside of it. Some of the windows are busted out, and the building is probably nine or ten stories high. In some places, it could be fifteen or twenty.

We pull up where a parking space could've been years ago, right by the door. There's another blacked-out SUV here. It has to be Lom. The painted lines that I'm sure were here many years ago are gone. Over the years, the elements must've taken the paint off.

Nal and I exit the vehicle and head for the two rusted-out green doors. He tries to pull it open for me, but I'm more than capable of doing it myself. I hold the door open for Nal, and the two of us head inside.

This doorway leads into the center of the warehouse where the main bit of the factory work must've taken place. The ceilings are hundreds of feet high and mostly made up of glass. In the center are two rows of ceiling fans at the very top, and that's the only part that isn't glass.

In the center of the room are a series of construction lights pointing at someone who's hanging by a chain. The chain is over a metal beam, and he's thrashing a good four feet off the ground. It has to be my stepfather. Nal and I approach, and the people surrounding Anzor turn around.

Lom, Nazyr, and Eset are who I recognize first, and then I spot another body. One I didn't know was here in the first place. It's Lom's right-hand man, Kirill.

"Brother! Now that you're here, I can start the festivities." Lom slaps his hands together, and it echoes throughout the vast space. I narrow my eyes because something feels off, and sure enough, Lom pulls out his gun and points it at Kirill.

Kirill seems taken aback by my brother's movements. He looks at Lom and then looks at me. "Anyone care to tell me what the meaning of this is?"

Lom doesn't hold back his smile. "Do you take me for an idiot? I know how Anzor got to the United States. You used our shipping company and smuggled him here. You paid off the port guard, and the port guard told me. No one goes against the Umarovas, Kirill. Surely you know this, and yet you acted stupid."

Kirill takes in a sharp breath and continues looking between Lom and me, then looks at Nazyr and Eset. "He took my daughter and promised she'd be returned to me once I got him here. None of us knew he was responsible for your capture, Ruslan. He took my daughter before you were out, and he still has her. He never came through with his end of the bargain."

Eset clears her throat and looks right at Kirill. "Knowing him, he probably already killed her. It's why he hasn't come through on his end of the bargain. My father only cares about one thing: himself."

Kirill's mouth falls open as my sister's words finally make him realize he's been played. "Where is the girl, Father?" Nazyr speaks up and asks the old man.

Anzor cackles and thrashes his arms against the chains. "Let me down, and I'll tell you."

"It doesn't matter where the girl is. Kirill betrayed us, and I will not stand for it. You were supposed to be loyal to me. You should have come to me when Anzor approached you. I could have helped you get out of this situation, Kirill, but now you leave me no choice." Lom pulls back the safety on the gun, and we all know what's about to happen. I don't intervene with my brother's business because Kirill was his second, the same way Danill is mine.

"No, please. My little girl could be out there somewhere. I don't know where she is! She needs someone!" Kirill pleads, and when I have my own children, I might understand the emotion in his voice. They say there is no greater love than the love a parent has for their child. Sadly, I've never experienced such love.

Eset takes a few steps forward, and with each step, her heels clack against the aged concrete. "If your daughter is alive, I will make sure she's found and that she's taken care of. What is her name?"

"Meryem," Kirill tells Eset. He clears his throat and then speaks again. "My family is dead. My parents and my late wife's. She died last year from an infection after she gave birth. Meryem only knows me, and without me, I fear for her."

"There is no reason to have fear. If she's still alive, I will make sure she's taken care of, but you betrayed my family, Kirill. You went against my brothers, and for that, you will pay the ultimate price." Eset runs her hand along Kirill's cheek and walks away. As she walks away, Lom pulls the trigger, and the bullet pierces his head, killing him instantly.

"This sucks. I liked him," Lom comments, shaking his head.

Laughter comes out from behind him, and Anzor's all smiles. "You've grown quite fierce, my little Eset. But why? You will be sold off to marry someone with more power. You know it, yes? Ruslan will arrange a marriage for you in an attempt to gain another ally. You are merely a bargaining chip to them, so why do you stand with them today? Hmm?"

Eset stops dead in her tracks and turns around. She glares at her father with the most might in the entire world. "I stand with them because I know what you did, and soon everyone else will too. You aren't my father. All you are is a sperm donor. You disgust me, pig. I hope you suffer greatly." Eset spits on her father and walks away from us before any of us can say a thing. I'm sure we could stop her, but I'm not sure I want to. It's obvious there's something she knows that I don't.

"You are a naïve bitch if you think they will protect you!" Anzor screams after Eset.

"We will protect her because she's our family," Nazyr comments, now taking his moment to speak up against his father.

"Family is disposable, boy. You'd do best to remember that. These two will throw you in the garden when I'm gone. You're a threat to them because you're my son and many people are loyal to me, not their name. People will seek you out to go against your brothers. They'll seek you out so you can start a new line in Chechnya."

"I'm loyal to my brothers, not to you," Nazyr screams at his father and pulls out his gun. He flicks back the safety and shoots him in the knee. Anzor releases a blood-curdling scream, and I smile at my brother with pride.

Nazyr and Eset might be his blood, but they're my blood, too, and I know they won't go against me.

"I should've had them kill you. You're too much trouble," Anzor hisses at me.

"I feel like I've heard that before," I remember the men in Armenia telling me I was too much trouble. I'm beginning to feel as though it's a compliment. I run my hand along my chin and look at Anzor. "Tell me, would it have been slow or quick?"

"Slow." He wastes no time answering, but little does he realize he's sealed his own fate.

"Perfect. Yours will be the same." I smile and look at my brothers. They both smile back for a moment, and then we shift to tight-lipped expressions. I have a few hours to kill before I have to be at Jordan Steeles, so I'm going to make it count.

Chapter Seventeen

Amelia

I planned on leaving the suite pretty early today, but Emily told me she had to go in to work unexpectedly for a few hours. Now I'm at the mall waiting for her, and it's just around dinner time. Danill's with me also, just as he always is.

 Sometimes Danill doesn't sit too close to me, but other times he's within a few feet. I can never really keep track of what he's doing. I like to think I'm trying to find some sort of method to how he works, just out of pure curiosity, but so far, I haven't figured it out.

 I'm sitting on a modern plush yellow chair in the middle of the mall. Mothers with kids whiz by me, and laughter fills the space. With the way online shopping's been in the last few years, I'm surprised malls are even still a thing. Now I'm not hating on them. I'd much rather go into a store and try on clothes as opposed to looking at something and clicking "add to cart". There's something different about trying on a little black dress and seeing how it looks in those dressing room mirrors.

 This mall's recently been renovated. I remember last year it was closed almost the entire time because they were having a complete overhaul. Now everything looks so much different. Before, it was bland, and there wasn't anything special about it. With the updates, they changed all the floors, added skylights throughout the walkway, and updated the storefronts within the mall. I like how they added the skylights. It really brightens the place up and makes it seem cozier and more inviting.

Suddenly, I'm grabbed from behind, and I jump. I immediately look at Danill, who seems amused, so I'm not worried in the least bit. I turn, and sure enough, it's Emily. "You're going to make me pee my pants one day."

"Oh, I'd kill to see that," Emily playfully jokes, and I smack her arm while I rise. "Sorry about having to change things up today. I thought I'd be off, but they called me in for a shift this morning into the afternoon."

Emily works part-time during the week at a local real estate agent's office. She said she was looking for some extra cash, and I let her know about a couple of openings at Illusion. As far as I know, Emily had an interview, and I want to see how that's going. "It's no big deal. Have you started at Illusion yet?"

Emily shakes her head, "No, not yet. I'm starting this weekend. Friday night's my first shift. You work Friday night, right?"

"Yep, I sure do. I think you'll like it there. The tips are great most of the time." I smile and walk alongside Emily. I don't think either of us had a specific store we wanted to go into, so I'm just walking with her.

"Perfect. I love having some extra cash. Wanna go in here?" Emily nods toward a small lingerie store. It's not comparable to Victoria's Secret because it isn't a name brand like that. It looks like something that someone local owns, not some major corporation.

"Sure, I could use some new pieces." I don't really have anything super sexy, so this'll be a good opportunity for me to grab a couple things to surprise Ruslan with.

We walk into the lingerie store, and bright white lights shine against dark espresso floors. In the center of the store are displays that have mannequins wearing average bras and panties. There are drawers on the displays arranged by size and color. Off to the right side, there's an athletic area and then an everyday cotton essentials area. On the left, there's the sexier stuff, from strappy lingerie to mesh items.

I've always thought the mesh stuff was super-hot, but I never indulged before. I head over to the mannequin with the cobalt blue mesh lingerie. I love how it's entirely see-through. It's like it gives you a sneak peek at what's to come. "You thinking about getting this one?" Emily inquires, and I shoot her a sly smile.

"Yeah, I think it would be really hot."

"It totally would, but I think the emerald green one would look so much better against your skin tone. You're tanner than I am, remember?" Emily laughs, and I look over at the green. It actually would look better on my skin, but there's a really vibrant electric purple too. I go over to that one and pull out my size. Purple it is.

Emily looks through the items in this section but moves over to the right, where it's a mixture of mesh and lace. It's sexy but also very feminine and pretty. She stops in front of a cherry red item. Now Emily isn't as tan as I am. She's a good bit paler, honestly.

"Who are you getting that for?" I cock a brow, and Emily gives me a knowing look. "It wouldn't be Lom, would it?"

"It might be." Emily laughs.

I want my cousin to be happy, but I have a feeling that Lom is such a player.

"Do you know if he'll be in town any time soon?" I think I remember Ruslan saying Lom was in the States, but I can't be too sure.

"I think he's in the States right now on business. I can't remember, though. I could be wrong. I can find out for you." I thought Emily and Lom exchanged numbers. She could just ask him herself, but it seems like she doesn't want him to know how much she's into him. I don't blame her. When I'm into a guy, I don't want him to know how much I like him, either. I think sometimes it makes them feel powerful, and they can act super dicky. We don't want to give guys too much; otherwise, their egos tend to show.

"If you wouldn't mind. He and I flirted a lot back in Grozny. If I ever had the opportunity, I'd like to see where things could go past a few intense make-out sessions. You know?"

I totally get what Emily's saying. I just hope she doesn't get hurt. I don't know much about Lom, but maybe I can ask Ruslan a little more about his brother.

As much as I want to let Emily do her own thing, I feel this intense need to warn her. "I don't know Lom well, but everything I've ever gathered about him leads me to believe he's a total player. I feel like he's the type who drags women along and then breaks their hearts."

Emily throws her head back and laughs as she makes her way down the racks. Now she's staring at a soft pink baby doll number. "Amelia, Lom isn't the first man I've ever had an interaction with. I might've grown up in Alabama, but I had my heart broken by way too many country boys. I've been around the block a time or two, and I know what to do to not get my heart broken again. I'm not looking for a relationship with him, but I'm expecting to at least get laid a couple times. I don't even expect any sort of relationship. He doesn't seem like he's the type who likes being tied down anyway."

Hearing Emily makes me breathe a little bit easier. The last thing I'd want is for her to hook up with my boyfriend's brother, and then there be some weird tension between all of us. Emily and I have gotten very close since she moved in with me, and I think there will be a lot of holidays when we're all together. That's the hope, at least. I just don't want any awkwardness because I plan on being with Ruslan for the long haul.

"Okay, sorry if that came across as weird."

"It didn't at all. You're worried about me, and it's adorable." Emily offers me a soft smile and pulls me in for a hug. The two of us embrace and continue to go around the store. We both find a couple more things and then check out. We head to another store that has a variety of clothes. Emily finds a few items, but I only grab a couple. Then we say our goodbyes and head home. She's going back to the apartment, but I'm heading with Danill back to the suite.

Within the hour, I'm back at the hotel with Danill, and we're walking inside. Ruslan's sitting on the couch, scrolling on his phone as I come in with Danill carrying my bags. "It looks like you had a successful girl's day with Emily." He's toying with me a bit, but I didn't go crazy with the shopping. I could've since he gave me his card, but I'd never do such a thing.

Danill sets the bags down on the table in the dining area, then disappears as usual. I go take a seat next to Ruslan and lean in for a kiss, which he happily obliges. "Did you have a fun day with your cousin?"

I nod, "Yeah. It was a blast, honestly. I don't think I've ever had a proper girl's day like that."

"Then you'll have to do it more. I'm glad you had fun. What did the two of you do?"

I shrug my shoulders. "Nothing too crazy. We met up at the mall and then went shopping. The real estate agent office Emily works at had called her to come into work for a few hours, so we only just left a couple hours ago. We went to a lingerie store and then to another apparel one."

"Lingerie, huh?" Ruslan raises both of his brows and looks over to the bags. I laugh and kiss his lips once more for good measure.

"You'll see them soon enough, don't you worry." As I finish speaking, Ruslan wraps an arm around me and holds me snugly against his body. For a few moments, I'm silent, and the more I think about it, the more I want to know about Lom. It feels like I need to know if Emily's going to get hurt, or at least what the chances are that she will.

"Why are you being so quiet? You must be thinking about something." Damn it. Ruslan knows me like the back of his hand.

"Emily sort of told me she has a crush on your brother, and she asked me if he was coming to visit soon. Now, I don't know a lot about him, but all I can think about is how much he reminds me of a player. I just don't want her getting hurt."

Ruslan sucks in a deep breath and looks at me. I can tell he's debating on telling me what I want to hear versus what's the truth. "Lom's always had one woman with him one day and another the next. From what I could tell back in Grozny, the two of them got a bit close. The entire time we were there, Lom was flirting with Emily. I haven't ever seen him do that before, so I'm not sure what to say. Besides, you can't control what happens. You have to let them figure it out for themselves."

As much as I want to be able to keep Emily from getting hurt, Ruslan's right. All I can do is let them figure it out for themselves.

Chapter Eighteen

Ruslan

I stayed the night with Amelia in the hotel suite, even though I could barely sleep. I think I was too amped up by everything that happened yesterday. I kept tossing and turning, wanting to head back to the old factory to confront Anzor. I didn't have to go there, but I kept thinking about how much I wanted to make him pay for what he's done. There isn't any time limit on making him suffer, but the desire to do so spreads across my body like an uncontrollable itch.

It's a little past one in the afternoon, and I spent some time here with Amelia before heading over to the factory. I told Danill and Nal to stay back with Amelia because I didn't need anyone tagging along with me. No one knows where Anzor is, and he's in a remote area. There's no threat being posed to me here, and honestly, I want my privacy with him. What happens today should only be witnessed by people within my family.

I remember how Anzor tried desperately to get Nazyr to go against Lom and me. He was trying to say we'd view him as a threat, but Nazyr isn't any threat to me. After it sunk in about his father's hand in my disappearance, Nazyr texted me and said he'd do whatever he needed to make things right. Deep down, I think Nazyr thought I'd be upset with him, but he wasn't the one who made the decision. Neither Eset nor Nazyr will be condemned for their father's mistakes. Other people might automatically kill them both for being his children because, in some twisted world, they could pose some sort of threat. I, however, will not be the one to kill my sister or brother.

I pull down the long driveway that leads to the factory and drive straight. Sure enough, Lom's blacked-out SUV is still there. I park beside his and get out of my vehicle, then head straight inside. The construction lights are still where they were yesterday, and my siblings sit around in chairs. Even Eset's here.

Anzor's feet now touch the ground, whereas they didn't yesterday. I furrow my brows and look at my siblings, unsure why he's given the luxury of using his feet to stand. "Who did this?"

No one says anything at first, and then Eset clears her throat and rises from her chair. "I did. He's been shot in both knees now, and I know it's excruciating to be putting any weight on them. I figured you'd be pleased with it, but instead, you seem upset."

I'm rendered speechless as I lick my lips. My sweet, innocent baby sister did this? Then again, yesterday, she proved she wasn't as innocent as she was when she was a child. I didn't realize Eset had the balls to shoot a gun, let alone her father.

My phone begins to ring, so I pull it out of my pocket. As soon as I see the caller ID, I have to laugh to myself. I bring the phone up to my ear and answer. "Mother, I didn't think I'd be hearing from you again."

"I know you have Anzor. You must let him go, Ruslan."

She has some nerve telling me what I need to do. "I don't have to do a damn thing, actually."

"He is my husband, and I demand you let him go!"

"You aren't my boss. I don't have to listen to a damn thing you say, mother. Anzor did unspeakable acts to me, and I'm done with this." As soon as I say Anzor's done unspeakable acts, Eset looks over to me. She hasn't said a word, yet I get the impression he's done far worse than I ever thought. There's something I don't know, but I will find out soon.

"Ruslan, if you do not let him go, I will never forgive you for this. I will not be your mother if you proceed with this madness!" Oh, so she wants to play that game. She wants to try to convince me that losing her isn't worth what I'm about to do to her husband. What a fucking joke. He deserves far more than I'm going to give him. If I could keep him here for the rest of his life and make him suffer, I would, but I have other things that require my attention.

"One day, you will thank me for setting you free from this madness. You might not think I noticed, but I saw the bruises that adorned your skin. I saw the way you'd tremble from him if he had too much to drink or if he raised his voice. You think the way he's treating you is okay, but it isn't. You're abused, mother. You think it's what you deserve, but it isn't. When you realize I've done you a favor, go ahead and reach out. In the meantime, goodbye." I hang up the phone without waiting to hear another word from her, slide the phone back into my pocket, and approach my stepfather.

He looks worse for wear. Dried blood coats his legs, and the bullet hole entrance wounds don't look too great. "She was trying to get me to let you go. It's laughable, really. You abused her for years, and she still feels like she owes you something. I wonder how you managed to get a woman like my mother and then how you made her fear for her life so much that she thinks she can't live without you." I shake my head. A mixture of disappointment in my mother and disgust with my stepfather washes over me.

"He brainwashed her. As a young girl, I didn't see it for what it was, but now I do. I don't know if you're aware, but I always looked up to you as a little girl. I thought you were the best father in the entire world, and then I started seeing more things. I never spoke about them because I knew it wasn't my place, but over the last few weeks, I found out so much. Do you want me to tell Lom and Ruslan what you did, Father?" Eset grows angrier by the second, and I don't understand why she's getting so furious.

"You think you know everything, don't you?" Anzor cackles and spits on Eset. "You're a dumb bitch, just like your mother. All you'll ever be good for is spreading your legs and giving children. There's nothing up there in that head of yours anyway."

Nazyr rises from his seat and heads straight for his father. He rears his fist back and slams it into his knee. Anzor thrashes against the impact and screams. Nazyr keeps punching his knees over and over again, and no one does a damn thing to stop him. None of us are fond of Anzor, not anymore, at least.

"I'll tell you what I discovered if the two of you wish," Eset speaks back up, looking at Lom and me.

I give her a nod, signaling her to go on.

"I don't know how to tell you both this, so I'm sorry for not knowing how to handle myself. When my father went missing, I thought something could've been wrong, so I tracked down old contacts of his to see what I could find out. It turns out he was perfectly fine, hiding away as he did many years ago. One of his old contacts got drunk and told me about the best murder of my father's life. I became curious, so of course, I had the man go on. After a few more drinks, I got the entire story out of him, how he killed your father, and then managed to convince our mother it was safer for her to remarry than it was for her to stay single. He told her she'd have a target on her back, that a single mother would be taken advantage of and wouldn't make it far."

All these years have passed, and no one was ever able to tell us who killed our father. The police couldn't even track down the person who did it.

"How do you know Anzor did it? He could've been hoping for some sort of bragging rights," Lom speaks up, and he could be right. There are a few details the two of us know about the case, about what was taken from our father's body after he was killed.

"The old man told me my father took an old coin from yours. He described it in great detail, and even the engraving on the back of it. He said every man in the Umarova family had carried it from your great-great-grandfather to your father. The man had said my father kept it hidden and even told me of the old place he used to hide it. It was in our family home, so of course, I went to look, and sure enough…" Eset digs into her pocket and pulls out a coin. I walk over to her, and she places it in my palm. I analyze the coin, and it's exactly what she said it is—it even has the initials. I know for a fact this was swiped from my father's body, as does Lom.

I can hardly believe this has happened. We finally have proof. Deep down, I suspected Anzor had some sort of hand in it, and it turns out he did.

I pull my gun from my holster, pull back the safety, and fire over and over again. I shoot in places that won't kill him, like his legs, arms, hands, and feet. I want him to suffer and to suffer greatly at that.

I wanted to kill him today. That was my original thought, but now I want him to suffer for a while longer. I'll leave him here for maybe a week, and every day I'll make sure he's in the worst pain of his life. I want him to be to the point where he's praying for death, and even then, I might not grant it.

Soon, Anzor will die, and it will be by my hand.

Chapter Nineteen

Amelia

It's a little past eleven, and Ruslan hasn't come back yet. Nervousness settles deep in my gut, and I do my best to refrain from freaking out. I throw the comforter from my legs and get out of bed, walking in my pajamas and fuzzy socks out to the main seating area.

I take a seat on the couch and pull the blanket that's thrown over the back of it over my legs. Everything looks as it should, and I wonder where he is. If he's running late, he usually sends me a text, or he might even call me. But today, he hasn't. I don't know what he's been doing over the last couple of days, but things have seemed a bit more tense for him. Not between the two of us, but like something is stressing him out.

Footsteps coming toward me cause me to glance up, and Danill fills my vision. "Miss Amelia, is everything all right?"

"Yes, Danill. I couldn't sleep, and Ruslan isn't home yet, so it's making me a bit worried." Ever since he went missing, I've been a bit more on edge. It's only natural, I suppose.

"He should be home shortly. He told me his obligations today kept him for longer than he thought they would."

I keep my eyes on Danill, and for some reason, I'm feeling a bit feisty. "And what sort of obligations keep someone until almost midnight?" I raise both of my brows and await some sort of answer, but I know Danill won't give me one. It's not his place to speak about Ruslan's business, and if I really want the answer, I'll have to ask Ruslan myself.

"That isn't my place to say, Miss Amelia," Danill tells me and offers me a sympathetic smile. His sympathetic smile doesn't make me feel better. It just aggravates me even more.

I bluster a sigh and rise from the couch. If I'm going to be this aggravated, I need a damn drink. I walk over to the small bar area and pull out a glass and bottle of tequila. There's an ice maker built into the bar, so I grab three cubes of ice and then pour the tequila over them. Once I'm finished, I put the tequila back from where I got it before I take a sip.

Just as I'm swallowing the tequila, I hear the distinctive sound of the elevator doors opening, and sure enough, more footsteps are coming my way. "Danill, I need you to head out to the factory and make sure Nazyr has another set of eyes on—" Ruslan pauses immediately when his eyes land on me as he rounds the corner.

I lean against the bar and take another sip. "Please, go on." There's no doubt about if I'm annoyed or not. It's pretty damn evident in my voice.

It's now I really take in what Ruslan looks like. His suit is a bit disheveled, and the first few buttons aren't together like they normally are. He has sweat lining his brow, and there are red splotches on what was a perfectly white dress shirt. He unbuttons the front of his suit and takes it off, hanging it over the back of a dining area chair.

"Danill, head to the factory and make sure Nazyr has help with Anzor. None of us are leaving him alone yet." Ruslan speaks to Danill but keeps his eyes trained on me. He unbuttons every button on his dress shirt and, once he's finished, pulls it off, then hangs it on the back of the chair as well.

"Certainly," Danill replies, and he heads down the hallway toward the elevator.

"Why are you getting home so late?" I can't stand here and act like I'm totally okay. I'm annoyed. I'm frustrated. I'm downright pissed. He has a phone, and he could've called or even texted me. Instead, he's let me fester in my emotions and get worried about him, and in my opinion, that's totally fucked up.

"I was handling some pressing business matters."

"Yeah, which totally explains the blood on your shirt," I snap at him, and Ruslan's taken aback by my quick-witted anger. I know he's involved in the crime world. He's told me that, but what he hasn't done is tell me exactly what's been going on these last couple of days. "I'm tired of being left in the dark. Especially over the last few days. You've been acting weird, and it's irritating the fuck out of me. There's so much secrecy, and there isn't any reason for it."

Ruslan nods a couple of times. "Yes, you're right."

"You've said we're together now, so you need to be more open and forthcoming with me, Ruslan. I'm never going to be a woman who sits back in the shadows and doesn't know what's happening. I'm your partner, not your enemy." Before Ruslan, I never felt worthy enough to know about these sorts of things. I probably wouldn't have ever spoken up before, either, but I am now.

"You're absolutely right. I owe you answers," I know this can't be easy for him either, but I'm glad he's making such an effort to be honest with me.

"Okay, so what's going on?"

"You know I was taken, but you don't know I found out who was behind my capture and torture."

I swallow hard at what he's telling me. He found who did this? Good! We'll make them pay greatly for everything he went through. God, who am I? I wouldn't have ever thought this way before, but so much has changed over the last few months. I suppose it's not necessarily a bad thing. I've become stronger because of it.

"Who's responsible?" I question, and Ruslan sucks in a sharp breath before answering me.

"My stepfather, Anzor."

I narrow my eyes, not understanding why his stepfather would orchestrate all of this. "What reasoning would he have?"

"So there's a bit of a background story I need to give you. You know I'm involved in the criminal world, but you don't have all the details. You know my name, Ruslan Umarova, and I gather you understand the Umarova name is where my family's power lies. My stepfather came into my life when I was merely ten years old, and my father was killed shortly before then. As the eldest son, it was my right to lead, but I was a child. My mother and stepfather agreed it would be best for him to take control of the family organization because I was so young."

"You were a child, and he had no place in speaking for you. He isn't an Umarova, correct?"

Ruslan smiles at what I've said. It has to be because I'm catching on quickly. "Correct. He has no ounce of Umarova blood in his body. He's an outsider, an outsider who methodically planned every move he made from my father's death to my capture."

My eyes go wide. Did he just say his father's death? "He killed your father?"

Ruslan nods once, and his expression grows more serious by the moment. "Yes. I only found out because of my sister, Eset. She was able to get the information I always wondered about. In the back of my mind, I had a theory he was responsible, but she got the hard proof he was. He planned it out, killing my father and then marrying my mother. He even took something off my father's body, something that was very important to the Umarova family. Eset looked around our family's estate and, sure enough, found the missing item safely tucked away."

God, this is horrible. It has to be awful to know your stepfather killed your dad, but there also has to be some sort of relief in finally having the answer too. "I am so sorry, Ruslan," I speak with the utmost sincerity, and he offers me a soft smile.

"There is nothing to be sorry for, *malen'kiy krolik*. I have the answers I always sought. And now I will make him pay for everything he's done."

"What will you do?" I'm not sure I'm ready for the answer he's about to tell me.

"I'm going to make him suffer in ways he's never dreamed of. He not only killed my father and put my life on a path that could've been avoided, but he also had me captured and tortured. Not to mention he beat my mother for most of their marriage. She even called me today and told me if I go forward with this, she isn't my mother anymore. She truly believes I'm the person in the wrong here, and that is a sad thing."

"You're going to kill him, aren't you?" My question even surprises me. Deep down, I think I already know the answer, but I want some sort of confirmation from Ruslan.

"Yes, I will. No one goes against my family or me and gets away with it. Just as no one will ever do the same to you. I won't let them, Amelia. Anyone who goes against my loved ones is also going against me." Ruslan's words take me by surprise a bit. I've known I'm important to him. That was made evident the other day when we had our heart-to-heart. Though, I didn't ever expect he'd go to such great lengths to keep me safe. Right now, at this moment, I realize Ruslan would kill for me if he had to.

I begin to break the distance between Ruslan and myself. He takes off the undershirt that was under his dress shirt. He lays it down on the back of the dining room chair and turns to face me as I come right up against him. "Thank you for doing everything you do for me."

Ruslan cups my face in his hands. "There's no need for thanks. I'd do it all again if I had to. For you, I'd do anything."

His words cause me to smile, but not in a happy way. It's more grateful for what he's doing. Thankful for having him in my life. I don't know what I'd do without Ruslan. My life could've been so different over the last few months. I could've been stressed and working my ass off, making no progress with my identity theft case. But because of Ruslan, we were able to figure out Carter's behind it all.

"You're like my dark guardian angel," I tell him, and a smile tugs at his lips.

"I like that. I will always make sure you are protected, Amelia. Forever and always."

I step closer to him and press my lips against his. Our kiss is soft and delicate, something I really need right now. I continue to kiss Ruslan, and his hands drop from my face down to my sides, pulling me flush against his body.

I pull my lips away from his and look up into his eyes. "Ruslan, I know what you said the other day… but I have to know. Are you serious about the money going in the past?"

Ruslan presses a chaste kiss to the center of my head. "The money means nothing to me, Amelia. You, on the other hand, are everything. I'm not ever going to hold you accountable for the money I paid Christian to get you out of that situation. I don't want there to be anything monetary between us. You're simply my woman, and I am your man."

Any residual heaviness I have left in me immediately leaves my body. We're both on the same page, and it feels so good to be here. I reunite my lips with his and kiss him with a feverish need. He runs his hands along my body, going down from my waist, over my ass, and skirting against my thighs.

Chills run up my spine, and I know we're about to take this to the bedroom. At least, I think we are. Ruslan brings his hands up over my hips and slides them under my silk pajama shirt. Ruslan breaks the kiss, and I suck in a breath in anticipation. He pulls it up and yanks it over my head, leaving me standing in front of him shirtless in just fuzzy socks and pajama bottoms.

He wastes no time hooking his thumbs under my waistband and doing the same thing to my bottoms, pulling them along with my thong until I'm solely standing in fuzzy socks. "You're so fucking beautiful, *malen'kiy krolik.*" His tone comes out hot and breathy, and I drop to my knees.

I've been thinking about this, about needing him in my mouth, for a couple of days. I love sucking his cock, and it makes me feel like such a whore when I think about it, but I don't care. There's nothing wrong with me wanting to be a sexy vixen with him. Not with the way he makes me feel.

I unbutton his pants, then unzip them. Tonight is going to be a long one, and I can't wait for how late he's going to continue to keep me up.

Chapter Twenty

Ruslan

Amelia and I spent most of the night caressing each other's bodies and bringing the other more pleasure than we'd felt in a long time. I find myself falling for this woman, and that's something I'm not used to. I think I might have told one other woman I loved her, but that love compared to what I feel for Amelia isn't even comparable. Is this what love should be? Is this what love should feel like? I think so, but I'm not too sure. All I know is that when I'm with Amelia, my entire life makes sense. I feel like I'm on top of the world, and nothing can knock me down.

I'm glad last night we spoke about things. It seemed like she really wanted to clear up what she is to me and what I am to her. It makes me think her feelings are growing just as strong as mine are. One day soon, I'll tell her how important she is to me, but I do think she has some sort of idea. It's not that I don't want to tell her how I feel. What I want is for all this madness with her ex and with my stepfather to be over with.

Amelia left this morning to go to her apartment with Emily. A place she barely goes to these days. Emily practically lives there alone, but I haven't brought up that fact to Amelia. I very much enjoy her warming my bed every night, and I don't want to give her a reason to head back to her apartment. She can go there whenever she wishes, but I've grown used to her being with me every night. After spending so much time without her, she's the one thing I craved more than anything else.

I'm almost at the factory now, and I did a lot of thinking during the night and through this morning. As much as I want to torture Anzor for as long as possible, I want to be done with him. All I want is for him to be a distant memory in the past, and soon he will be.

I just got off the phone with Jordan Steele a few minutes ago. I did end up going to his house in his gated community for dinner. When I arrived, I met the rest of his children along with his lovely wife, Lacey. She's a Latina woman who's obviously the one who wears the pants in the relationship. At one point during the night, she asked him to do something, and he told her he'd be there in a minute. The look she shot him was enough for hell to freeze over.

The night went well, and we finalized the contracts. Jordan's niece Leona was there, and it looked like she was either learning how these sorts of contracts work or drawing them up herself. Within the contract, I found they wanted more shipments than what we originally discussed the other day. It was a good surprise, and one Jordan didn't authorize with me beforehand. He didn't even ask if I had that type of inventory reserved for him, but he's obviously my highest-paying client, and I'll do whatever I can to keep him happy.

I arrive at the factory by myself and park where I typically do. I head inside the same metal doors, and sure enough, my entire family is there again. Last night Nazyr watched over his father along with Danill, but this morning Lom and Eset came back. Though, I'm a bit surprised to see Nazyr is still here. He's asleep in a chair, but nonetheless, he's here. I wonder why he hasn't left, but knowing him, he doesn't want to miss the good stuff.

"Brother, how'd you sleep?" Eset asks as she rises from her seat and comes to hug me.

I wrap my arms around her and kiss her on the forehead. "Well, and you?"

She shoots me a serious look. "With everything going on, I couldn't really sleep."

It's the first time she's ever had to deal with something like this, and it's her first step within the crime world. I wasn't even going to offer Eset a spot at the table yet, but she's walked right up to it, and I won't be the one to take it away from her. The last thing I'll do is make her feel like her father could be right… like she's just some sort of bargaining chip for my power.

"It will get easier as more time passes. In the beginning, it's rough, but over time you get used to it." I'm not sure if my words will help her, but I wish when I first started in this world, someone had given me some sort of reassurance.

I glance past my sister and look at my stepfather. He's hanging by chains wrapped around his wrists, and his feet are touching the ground. There's a mixture of dried-up and fresh blood across his entire body. The bullet holes are gaping in his skin, and there's still blood that oozes from his wounds. There are now cuts along his torso and legs that weren't there yesterday when I was here.

"Did he do something to piss someone off?" I question, looking at the rest of my siblings.

"Yeah." Lom cackles and glances over at Eset.

"What? I'm getting really tired of being told I'm only useful for my vagina. Does it look like I'm just a walking breeder? No. Look at him. I can handle myself," Eset grumbles at the rest of us.

Lom's getting a kick out of it while I'm impressed with my sister's strength. A strength I didn't even know she had. Out of everyone, Eset's really proven herself to me. Most would condemn me for even offering Nazyr and Eset anything, but I will come to them with some position. I think Eset could do a great job securing deals and going to public events where our family needs representation. She's quick-witted, strong, and good on her feet. She'd, of course, have some a guard with her, but I could see her doing very well with a job like that.

"He won't be here much longer. His heart rate's been dropping, and he's growing paler by the hour," Nazyr speaks up, but there isn't an ounce of disappointment in his voice. I wonder if he, too, feels bad for what his father did to Lom and me. Nazyr and Eset had their father growing up, but everything that's come to light over the past few weeks has to have played some role in their lack of emotion. Granted, they probably held some sort of emotion at first. I remember when I dropped the bomb on them, they did have emotions, but I don't think either of them was really surprised. If they dug down underneath the surface, I bet they expected their father to be this foul.

"There is something I want to know before I kill you," I state as I approach Anzor. He flutters his eyelids open, and I can see how close to death he really is. He's as close as Nazyr said. If we're lucky, he'll make it another couple of hours. "Why did Artos betray me? How did you get one of my longest friends to turn against me?"

Anzor cackles, but it sounds strained. He hasn't been given water since he's been here, and his voice is gravelly. "Artos was loyal to me as head of the family. He appeased you, boy. Everything the two of you ever spoke about was told to me. He was loyal to me as head of the family, not you. You're a fraud pretending you have the power here. I still have the power, and you will see it after my death. People will plot against you and turn against you all in my name. I can't wait for everything you think you have to be burned to the ground." Anzor smiles in a sinister manner, and I'm done playing these games. I'm done with him thinking he has some sort of power over me when at the end of the day, he was the fraud. He's always been the fraud.

I go over to Eset and hold out my hand. "The knife you used. I need to borrow it."

Eset pulls up her pant leg and reveals a strap with a knife as long as the bottom part of her leg. She hands it to me, and I walk up to my stepfather. "I've really grown tired of your voice," I say to him as I jab the knife straight into his throat, piercing his vocal cords. He gurgles on the blood, and I smirk as the fear rolls across his face. He wants to get out of this, but there's no turning back.

I pull down on the blade and yank it as far as I can until I hit his chest bone. He continues to choke on his own blood, and I know I could stop here, but I won't, not after everything he's done to my family and me. I pull the blade from his body and decide to go into his sides. I want to pierce his lungs, so I slam the knife in as deep as it'll go on the right side behind his ribs and then do the same to the opposite. He thrashes against the chains and then slowly comes to a stop.

I step back and look over his tired, worn-out body. I watch and wait for some sort of breath, sound, or any signal of life. But there isn't one. There isn't one damn thing. I sigh in relief, knowing I'll no longer have to deal with Anzor, and neither will my brothers or sister. We're all finally free.

The four of us go over to the chairs that have been here the last few days, and all take a seat. Nazyr doesn't say anything, and neither does Eset. I think it's finally sinking in that they're free as well.

"What does this mean now?" Nazyr questions, and Lom looks at me.

"It means Ruslan is in charge, and we have a fresh start." I nod at what Lom's saying.

"We have a new age coming. A new opportunity for the family, and most won't understand what I want to do. They'll judge me for it, say I'm bringing two people who are enemies too close to me… but you are my siblings, and I want you to have roles within the organization. I don't know how yet, but I will come up with jobs for the two of you if it's what you want," I pause for a moment and gauge their reactions, but there is one thing I need to make clear. "Eset, I think you know I'd never condemn you to what your father would. If you're part of the family, you won't have a marriage contract arranged for you. You will have actual duties and a significant role to play."

Eset smiles at me and nods in thanks. "I'd like that very much, brother."

"And you, Nazyr, what do you say?"

"I say I've come along on the ride this far. I'm ready to see it through." I smile at Nazyr's comment, and Lom looks at me with a serious expression crossing his face.

"Why are you looking at me like that? Tell me what's on your mind," I order him, and Lom wastes no time telling me exactly what he's thinking.

"Do you plan on staying here in Atlanta?"

"I'm not sure. Why?"

"No one will take you seriously as the head of the family if you stay here. Anzor was in power for so long. They're going to want someone who's present. If you aren't present, I'm afraid of what could happen." He thinks the entire order of power could fall if I'm not there, and it's an excellent concern to bring up.

Things aren't as simple as they were before. I don't feel like I can just get on a plane tonight and return home. It isn't just about me now. I have Amelia, too, and what she wants in life matters to me.

"We will do whatever we can to hold things over until you make a decision or can come back home," Nazyr speaks up, and I give him a nod in thanks.

"Yes, we will do what we can. What do you want done with his body?" Eset asks, and it surprises me that she's the one asking this.

I've thought about this long and hard. "I want him beheaded and his head to be displayed in the center of Grozny. His body can be burned here in the woods for all I care. Anzor will be an example of why not to cross the Umarova family."

"When we arrive back home, we'll begin searching high and low for Artos. He will be the next one we make an example of," Lom says, and I nod in agreement. Some days I feel like he can read my mind.

This day has been a long time coming. Now all I have left to do is tie up a few loose ends. Artos and Carter are high on my priority list, and then maybe I can leave and go back to Grozny, with Amelia, of course.

Chapter Twenty-One

Amelia

Ruslan was only gone for a few hours before he came back to the hotel suite. Once he got back, he went straight into the shower. He didn't even say a word to Danill or me. Nal has been off on some sort of assignment. Part of me thinks Ruslan told Nal to track down Carter, and deep down, I think I'm right.

I head into the kitchen and grab two slices of bread, tie up the bread container, and then go to the fridge. I grab some butter and a pack of cheese slices.

I've really been craving a pan-fried grilled cheese, so I'm going to make myself one today. I grab a pan from the cupboard and go ahead and head up to the stove. I'll give it a few minutes to warm the pan before I put the bread in it.

I butter the bread and tuck two slices of cheese between them when my phone starts ringing on the counter. I have just enough time to plop the sandwich down in the pan and answer the phone. "Hello?" I say into it, without even looking to see who it was.

"Hey, are you busy?" It's Emily, and she sounds a little frazzled.

"Not really. I'm just making a grilled cheese sandwich."

"Oh, okay. Um, well… your mom showed up at the apartment. She was banging on the door like a mad woman, and I had to let her in, or the neighbor was going to call the cops. She's..." In the background, I can hear my mother asking Emily if I'm on the phone and when I'm coming over. My mother sounds so different, and there's a desperation in her voice I've never heard before.

"She's not like herself, Amelia. Can you come over and see what's wrong? I... I have a theory, and I'll text you about it," Emily whispers the last bit, and I can sense how uncomfortable my cousin is right now. She doesn't want to be alone with my mother, and while I don't know why, I'm going to find out.

"Yeah, I'll be there in thirty minutes. Okay?"

"Yep, sounds good. Hurry if you can."

Emily and I quickly say our goodbyes, and while I flip my sandwich over, I call out for Ruslan. He comes out of the bedroom and walks up to me. "That smells good. What is it?"

"It's a grilled cheese sandwich, but that's not why I called you in here. My mother showed up at the apartment, and Emily's keeping her there. Em sounds like she needs our help."

Ruslan comes over to me and shuts off the stove, then moves the pan over to a burner that isn't hot. "All right, then let's go." Ruslan takes my hand in his and waves Danill to come with us. We all head out of the suite, go down the elevator, and rush to the SUV as quickly as possible. Ruslan even drives like a madman as he speeds through Atlanta to get to the apartment.

We're there in no time, and my heart is beating intensely in my chest with every waking moment. I don't know why my mom would show up out of the blue. She's never done this before, which makes me feel like she's losing it. She only ever needs me for some money or something, so I have to figure out what's going on.

Before the car's even parked, I throw open my door and get out. Danill follows close behind me since Ruslan's driving, and he's hot on my heels as I approach the door. I place my hand on the knob and turn it, pushing it open with intense speed. There's this gut-wrenching feeling I have like something isn't right.

Emily's sitting on the couch, tapping her fingers on her knees nervously, and my mother's pacing around the living room. If that isn't nerve-wracking enough, the gun in her hand adds to it. "I don't know why he'd do this to me. It doesn't make sense." My mother smacks herself on the forehead and repeats how he did this to her, over and over again.

"Mom…" I say her name, trying so hard not to let there be any inflections in my voice. I don't want her to know I'm afraid right now, but I am. Footsteps come from behind me, and Ruslan fills the doorway.

My mother looks me up and down. "Amelia!" She waves her hands around and points the gun in the air. I don't know if it's real or not. These days they have fake guns that look like the real thing, but all they shoot are BB pellets.

"Mom, what's going on? I wasn't expecting you." I try to act nonchalant, and it's taking everything in me not to freak out right now.

"I know you weren't. Yes, I know you weren't." She shakes her head and does it a couple of times. "Yes, you were. You should've known I'd come here for you. We need to talk." She stops speaking and stares at me blankly. "You're hiding him. Aren't you?" My mother charges for me, but Danill steps in between the two of us and knocks the gun out of her hand. It falls on the floor a couple of feet away from my mother, and Emily gets up and grabs it so my mom can't get it.

Ruslan shuts the door behind him and locks it while Danill pulls my mother's hands behind her. He'll hold her because she can't be trusted right now, and I'm grateful for it. Now that Danill's holding her arms back, the red and brown speckles along her arms are undeniable. She's been using. Heroin, if I had to guess.

"Who are you talking about?" I ask her, and she stares at me like I actually know. Her eyes go wide, and she shakes against Danill's grip.

"Don't act stupid! Where's Carter? Why hasn't he given me my money! That was the deal! He was supposed to give me money for what I did. He wasn't at that damn motel either."

Ruslan takes a step forward and stands beside me. "What motel would that be?"

"The yellow one with the red sign right off the interstate. It's next to the taco place. He's been staying there for a couple months, but he wasn't in his room! I went looking too. He said he'd give me my money, but he didn't. He's a no good, lying, dirty bastard! After all that work too. I gave him everything he needed, and he didn't pay me! I want my money, Amelia! I want my money! You need to tell me where he is right now 'cause I'm gonna shake him down, and he's gonna give me my money." My mom screams at the top of her lungs, and then out of nowhere, she stops, collects herself, and looks at me. "Can I borrow forty bucks, Amelia bug? I'll pay you back. I just need to get something really quick. I need my medication."

Medication? More like her drugs. I shake my head and stand firm with her. "I don't know where the fuck Carter is, but just like you, I'd like to know. And no, I'm not giving you forty bucks so you can shoot that junk into your veins. Look at yourself, Mom. God, Dad would be so disappointed."

My mother manages to wriggle free from Danill's grasp and tries to strike me, but Ruslan steps in front of me. My mother ends up hitting him, and Ruslan grabs her by the wrists and pins her up against the wall. "Don't you ever try and hurt Amelia again. If you do, it'll be the last thing you ever do. Mother or not, I don't care. No one hurts her."

"Amelia! This crazy bastard is trying to hurt me!" my mother repeatedly screams, like I'm going to save her, but I won't.

Danill walks over to where Ruslan is and takes over, holding my mother against the wall. Ruslan comes back over to me, and I scan over his body and make sure he's okay. There's a slight tinge of redness, but nothing more than that.

"You want me to help you? Tell me what Carter owes you money for." She's delirious enough that she might just do it.

"Okay, yeah, yeah, I can do that. That nasty boyfriend of yours owes me money 'cause I helped him. I helped him real good. I got him some information so he could make some quick money!"

I blink a couple of times and know I need more information. "What kind of quick money, Mom?"

"Oh, you know, the kind for credit cards and stuff. He said he was going to get you out of here and build a new life for you. All he said he needed was some information like where you were born, your social, and your first pet's name. There was some other stuff, too, but I gave Carter everything you needed to start that life. He said he was gonna pay me real good for what I gave him, but he never did, and now I'm out of money. I can't survive out there, Amelia. I'm sleeping in a tent, and I really need forty dollars. Please, can I have forty bucks?"

Looking at my mother, I feel a mixture of betrayal, hurt, anger, and disappointment. She's how Carter got all the information to properly steal my identity. He saw her for what she was, a desperate woman who needed money and used that to his advantage. She's standing here in dirty, torn clothes, looking like she hasn't brushed her hair in weeks. She needs more than forty dollars. She needs a lot more than that to even make some sort of decent dent in her life, but I'd never ask Ruslan to help her like this.

Not after I found out that she's how Carter gained access to all my personal information. Here I thought he picked the lock to my box with my social, birth certificate, and bank information. Lo and behold, it was my mother.

"Mom, I don't know why you came here with a gun and tried to steal from me, but I'm calling the police right now," I say, and my mother starts screaming in the background. I pull my cell out of my pocket and call the non-emergency line, then explain what I said to my mother a few moments ago.

I don't want the police to think she showed up with a gun in an attempt to shake me down. I'm going to make them think she's high as a kite, and she tried to steal from me to feed her habit. She had my poor cousin as a hostage until we got there and were able to get the gun from her grasp.

Within ten minutes, two officers show up, take statements from the four of us, and then put my mother in the back of their squad car. She wants to scream and shout about Carter owing her money, but the officers don't know who Carter is. When they ask me, I tell him he's an ex-boyfriend who hasn't been in my life in a long time and that my mother's habit's gotten out of control.

The officers tell me because of the extent of her crime, she'll likely be doing jail time, and the judge probably won't let her go to rehab. As cold as it might sound, I want her to go to jail. It's what she deserves.

Then I get to thinking about it, and she deserves far, much worse than jail time. She's lucky I have a conscience.

Chapter Twenty-Two

Ruslan

This afternoon took a very unexpected turn when Amelia's mother confessed to playing a role in Amelia's identity theft case. Throughout the entire scenario, I was blown away by how Amelia handled herself. She did what she had to do, even though I knew there was a part of her that probably wanted to ask me if we could send her to rehab.

I have no doubt Amelia loves her mother, but when someone so close to you betrays you like that… you can't help but want them to pay for what they've done.

Her mother did give us some good information about where to look for Carter, so I sent Nal and Danill out on the streets to see what they could find out. Nal decided to have somewhat of a stakeout, and he was right in doing so. As a newer person on my team, he's quick on his feet and has a good head on his shoulders. There aren't too many people I'd keep on my team for life, but Nal has potential, as Danill did back in the day. I asked Danill his thoughts on Nal, and he has the same opinion of him: he's young, smart, and quick.

Nal ended up figuring out Carter was staying at the same motel, but at some point, he switched rooms. My guess is he knew Amelia's mother was looking for him, and he still wanted to keep a low profile, so he asked to change his room to one on the other side of the motel. Amelia's mother might not have even looked on the other side. She probably thought he just up and vanished, but I know that isn't the case.

When Nal and I saw Carter a couple weeks ago, he was at a house, not at this motel. It made me curious if Amelia's mother was right or if she was merely a desperate woman looking for her next fix. Sure enough, I arrived at the motel with Danill while Nal was watching Carter's room. He's been in the room since around five, and it's seven now. I found out from a lovely lady at the front desk that Carter has, in fact, rented this room for a few weeks, so Amelia's mother wasn't talking out of her ass.

I'm still in the motel's office with Danill, speaking to Sherry, the woman working at the front desk. "Is there anything else you can tell me about what Jack's been up to?" Carter gave them a fake name because, of course, he would. He didn't want to get caught, and he did a decent job of it.

"Yeah, there are some people who show up late at night. They always have bags. I don't know what's in them, but some of his neighbors have come up here complaining they don't want to be anywhere near a drug dealer." Shirley raises both of her brows and seems a bit concerned. "But you know, I can't control what kind of people come to the likes of this place. It's not exactly the nicest joint in town, ya know?"

"Of course. I'll take a look into it for you, and in the meantime, you go out and spoil yourself a little bit." I dig into my pocket and pull out five hundred dollars for Sherry, then slide them over to her.

"Are you sure, Mr. Kilgore?" I also gave Sherry a fake name because in the event people go looking for Carter, I'm not going to take the fall for it. I'll do whatever I need to protect myself and the people who love me.

"I'm sure. Thank you for all of your help, Sherry," I assure her and walk out with Danill. We get in the SUV, and he pulls it around to the other side of the hotel where Carter's room is. I wonder if he was using both the house and this motel room as drop-off points for drugs. The more my mind wanders, the more I think he could've used the money he stole from Amelia to fund his drug business. It would make sense from what Sherry told Danill and me, but I'll only find out once we get Carter in our hands.

We walk up to the entrance, and Nal gets out of his SUV to meet us. I grab onto the motel door handle and use my body weight to pop the door free. Carter's lying back on the yellow-colored bed and jumps up. "Who the fuck do you think you are?"

I shake my head and scoff at him. "Don't you recognize my voice, Carter? I might get offended if you don't."

Carter immediately stills. "I left her alone. That's what you said I had to do."

I nod a couple of times. "Yeah, that was before I found out you're the one who stole her identity or that you took advantage of her mother's illness to get the information you needed. It takes a pretty fucked up person to use an addict's vice for their own personal need. Now, I think I have most of the picture put together, but there are a couple of fuzzy parts here. Do you care to clear them up, or are we going to do this thing where you say you don't know what I'm talking about?"

"Boss," Danill speaks up and nods to the right side of the room. There are three trash bags semi-tied off, so I motion for Nal to go over and check them out. Sure enough, he walks over and opens the bags. Two of them are packed with bags of weed, and another one of them is a white powder. He did use the cash to start a business with cheap weed and shitty coke.

"Never mind. Looks like I have the answer I need. Nal, take that shit with us." Nal picks up the bags at my command, and Danill pulls out his gun and goes over to Carter. Not surprisingly, Carter drops to the floor on his knees.

"Please don't kill me. I'll give back all of the money. I promise. I'll fuckin' do it, man. It's not worth my life."

Danill cackles in his face. "You should've thought about that before you stole from Miss Amelia." Danill whips his gun back and slams it against Carter's head. Carter's body drops to the floor, and Danill makes sure he's really out before he picks him up in his arms.

"Where are we headed, boss?" Nal asks.

"The factory the Steeles have. It's remote enough to do what we need, and we can stash the shit there until we can get it tested. If it's usable, I want to get it onto the streets and make some money back for Amelia," I tell Nal, and he nods.

The group of us head out to our SUVs, and then we get on the road. It takes about forty minutes to get out to the factory from where the motel was, but I don't much care about how long it takes. It could've taken us four hours, and I would've been patient as hell because Carter's finally in my grasp.

We get to the factory, and Nal brings the bags inside. Danill's carrying Carter, and I walk beside them. Nal takes the bags to one area while Danill drops Carter to the ground. He drops him in the area where my stepfather's fresh blood is still drying. I can't wait to see his face when he wakes up.

Danill and I sit down in the chairs and wait for Carter to stir awake. Meanwhile, I send Nal on a job to get some equipment to test the product. If it's good, I'll make money off it. If it isn't, it's money down the drain, and I'll make Carter suffer even more. Who am I kidding? I'm going to make him suffer as much as I can either way. He screwed with the wrong woman. He caused her immeasurable pain and suffering. For that, there isn't enough pain I can give him.

Another thirty minutes pass by before Carter begins coming to. He blinks a few times and runs his hand along the blood-stained cement. Once his eyes open, they widen, and he looks around like a scared child being cornered by bullies. He brings his hands up to his legs, and the red stains cause him to breathe in and out faster. "W-what is this?" he stutters.

"Come on, Carter. Surely you know what that is."

It takes a few seconds, but it finally sinks in, and Carter swallows hard. "I didn't follow her anymore. I left. I left to leave her alone."

"That's the thing. You didn't leave to give Amelia space. You left because you feared what we'd do when we found it all out."

"Idiot," Danill adds, and Carter looks between the two of us.

"Who are you? I've never seen you in my life, and I was with Amelia for a long-ass time."

"I'm your worst fucking nightmare, Carter." I rise and go up to him. I grab him by the back of his scraggy hair and pull as hard as I can. "You screwed with the wrong woman. She has people who care about her. People who will make sure your death isn't as quick as you'd hope."

"No, man, come on. I did what you said! I left her alone."

"After you already ruined her life, right? That's the part you're forgetting, you slimy piece of shit!" I roar into his face and throw him onto the ground. There's a sledgehammer a few feet away, so I head over to it, lean down, and pick it up.

It's a bit heavier than I thought it would be, so I swing it around a few times for good measure and then aim for Carter's leg. I slam it down with as much strength as I have, and a crackling sound rings out around us. While Carter screams bloody murder, I'm smiling, as is Danill.

There's nothing sweeter than seeing someone suffer who deserves it. "You're doing this for my sloppy seconds?" Carter begins cackling like a madman in a desperate attempt to throw me off my game. "She's used up, no good, disgusting even. You're fucking her, right? You'll grow bored of her one day soon. I sure did."

I shake my head and don't bother replying to him. He's not worth it. I bring up the sledgehammer again and crash it down against his shoulder. It pops free from his socket, and he's slowly looking like the hunchback of Notre Dame. I bring the hammer back again and do the same thing to the other side.

"She's just a washed-up whore." Carter begins cackling, and after a few seconds, I realize he can see my anger all across my face.

"Danill, Nal! Get over here." Both of my men come up to me. "Hold him down." They both do as I say, and they shove him to the ground, laying him flat on his back. I wanted to take a good bit of time doing this myself, but where I actually want to be is back with Amelia.

They're holding him down at his shoulders, and I walk around his body, standing over his head. I line the sledgehammer up with his head, pull it as high as I can in the air, and then slam it down. With one hit, his skull cracks into many pieces. Brain matter oozes from his forehead, and his mouth is now a gaping hole.

Danill and Nal both let go of Carter, and I slam the sledgehammer down over and over again. Eventually, Danill comes up to me and pulls on my shoulder. He's only seen me become a savage a few times, and this time I had good reason.

Carter hurt Amelia badly, and I wasn't going to let him have an easy death. "I'll handle the body. You go back to Miss Amelia, boss," Danill says.

I look over at him and give him a nod in thanks. "Make sure nothing can be traced back. Pull every tooth from what's left of his skull and burn him until he's nothing but ash."

"You got it, boss."

I know Amelia's at the mall with Emily right now to destress, but as soon as she gets home, she and I need to have a conversation. I need her to come back to Grozny with me, and if she doesn't want to go, I might very well throw her over my shoulder and make her.

Chapter Twenty-Three

Amelia

"I can't believe what happened earlier. I mean, it feels like we're in some sort of movie or something." Emily shakes her head in disbelief as she sips her coffee. I'm in shock, too, but not just because of what happened earlier at the apartment.

We ended up staying there for a little bit after the police were done questioning us. Danill and Ruslan had already made sure I was okay, but then they were checking on Emily. I had gone to the restroom, and there wasn't any toilet paper, so I went below the sink to get some. Then I was staring at a pregnancy test. I'd always kept them in the bottom of the cabinet just for those months when I was terrified there might be an accidental pregnancy. I was always lucky in the sense my periods were just a few days late, probably because of stress. Only, as I was staring at that pregnancy test, I realized I was two weeks late, not just a couple days.

So, what did I do? I peed on the test and almost passed out when I saw 'pregnant' on the screen. "Amelia, are you okay?" I glance up at Emily and don't think I heard her right.

"Sorry, what did you say?"

"Um... I asked if you were okay. You're acting weird, being all quiet and stuff." Emily takes another sip of her coffee while I haven't even touched mine.

"I'm pregnant," I blurt out, and Emily practically chokes.

"Wait. What?"

"I'm pregnant, Emily. I just found out, and I'm..." I can't even finish my sentence.

"You're in shock, naturally." Emily puts the pieces together, and I nod. "Does Ruslan know?"

I shake my head. "No, I haven't had a second to tell him."

"Shit, you mean you *just* found out?"

"Yeah, as in, within the last four hours found out. I'm still processing it. Like, should I even be drinking this right now because I don't know?" I stare at the coffee in front of me, wondering if it'll immediately kill a baby if I take a sip. God, I've been drinking. What kind of mother am I going to be?

"Okay, take a breath. You can have one cup of coffee a day. I know that for a fact. So drink the coffee. You deserve it after the day you've had." I pick up the iced coffee and take a sip. I shut my eyes as the vanilla flavoring coats my tongue.

"This wasn't planned, and I'm low-key freaking out. What is Ruslan going to think? What if he doesn't want this? I keep thinking about so many things, and I'm becoming so worried. He wanted me. He's never once told me he wanted a family, and my worst fear is that he won't want this."

Emily grabs my hand from across the table and gives me a reassuring squeeze. "Ruslan isn't going to abandon you because you're pregnant. I haven't been around the guy too much, but he's absolutely head over heels for you. One day, I hope to find a man that looks at me the way Ruslan looks at you. It's what every woman wants, Amelia. You have it right at your fingertips, and I'm sure when you tell him, he's going to be shocked, but he's going to be so happy. Unless... do you want to terminate it?"

I shake my head. "No, I don't think I could stomach the idea of doing that. Not that I'm blaming women who choose it. I just... I can't do that."

"Okay, well, no one is forcing you." As soon as she says it, my thought immediately drifts to what if Ruslan asks me to. "He's not going to ask you to do it, and you know it."

God, it's like she can read my fucking mind. "I know. Everything is so fresh, and I feel so confused, I guess."

"You're mind-fucked right now, and that's totally okay. If it were me, I'd be mind-fucked too."

"Well, with you, it would make sense since you never screwed Lom, right?" I raise both of my brows and stare at her.

Emily nervously laughs. "I never fucked him back then, but we got close… really close."

"So, what happened with that? It's not like you to turn down something when you're feeling it."

"I wasn't the one who turned it down. He said it wouldn't be a good idea, given how close you are with his brother. He said he didn't want to create any sort of drama between all of us. I told him we were adults, and he said we were and that if we saw each other again and the connection was still there, we could explore it. It's why I've been texting him so much, I think… because I really want that connection to stick because I like him. I… I did screw him the other day, though."

I haven't ever known Emily to be really into a guy. I remember she did date some boys from back home, but like she's told me before, they're heartbreaking country boys. They weren't the type who cherished your heart. They're the ones who want in your pants and don't give a fuck if they leave you alone to pick up the pieces when they're done with you.

"What do you mean you screwed him the other day?"

"He's here, in the States. We met up for a booty call, I guess, and it was phenomenal. It was so freaking good, and he's still texting me and everything like normal. I think he might see we do have some sort of connection." They might have a connection, but Lom lives in Grozny. What's going to happen when he goes back and Emily's here?

"How many more months do you have left with your program?"

Emily sucks in a deep breath, "About seven if I keep up with the same workload I have now. I could double up some courses and get done in five, but I think it would fry my brain." So she has seven more months of being stuck in Atlanta.

"Does Lom know you have to stay here? Like, you can't just hop on a flight and go to Grozny whenever you want?"

"No, because he hasn't even asked. We're not dating. We're just… friendly people who enjoy each other's company every once in a while."

"Ah, is that what you're doing?" I laugh at Emily and finally feel myself getting a bit more carefree. I'm not focusing on being a pregnant woman right now, and all the worries I have are slowly fading away. The more I think about it, the more I know Emily's right. It's not like Ruslan's going to be mad at me about anything. I'm sure he'll be shocked at first, too, and then he'll probably be happy. I'll still be a nervous wreck until I actually get a moment to talk to him about it, though.

"Yeah, I am." Emily playfully shoves my hand away, and we both break out into laughter. "On another note, you're going to be the best mom in the world. I hope you're not nervous about that."

"I am, but not in a scary sort of way. Nervous because it's such a big change, but I'm ready for more change. Look at the last few months. All my changes have been good ones, and it's put my life on this road to happiness. A road I never expected to be on, honestly."

"You deserve it. If anyone deserves it, it's you. You've been through so much. God, when you lost your dad, it broke my heart. I know you loved him more than anything else in the world. Then your mom started drinking and using to cope with her loss. I know how hard you tried to keep her on a straight path. You tried so hard, Amelia, and no one blames you for eventually turning a blind eye to what she was doing. I would've done the same thing if I was in your shoes."

No one ever understands that part of my life. Everything was perfect when my father was alive, but when he died, my mother lost a big part of herself. I think she didn't know how to survive without him. Actually, I take that back. She didn't know how to live her life without him. What she's doing now is surviving, but she's barely surviving.

"Thank you for always being here for me." I reach over and grab Emily's hand one more time and give it a squeeze.

"Always. And I think it's so weird we're here alone. Ruslan always has someone watching you, right?"

I nod, "Yeah, he always does, and he knew exactly where I was going with you," I tell her and scan the food court. I look for what I know organized crime members wear, which is usually some sort of suit. Sure enough, my eyes land on Lom with another man and a woman beside him. "You know, you're pretty damn lucky you weren't facing my direction."

"Huh, why?"

"Because your lover boy is back there watching us and can probably read my lips." I wiggle my eyebrows, and Emily turns around and scans the food court. Sure enough, she looks straight ahead, and Lom smiles the second she sees him. It's cute, and I hope for my cousin's sake that she doesn't get hurt, but she's a big girl and can handle herself.

"Are you done with your coffee? There's something I need to do, and I'd really like you to tag along with me if you don't mind." Emily turns around to face me as I speak and nods.

"Yeah, where are we going?" she asks.

"Illusion. I need to speak to Gregor or Christian. I'm going to put in my two weeks' notice since I'm pregnant. I highly doubt Ruslan wants me working at a club while his child's growing inside me. Now, I know you picked up a couple of shifts a week from there. Would you be opposed to taking my three days a week? This way, they're not freaking out about finding someone to fill my spot."

"I make more money there than in the real estate office, so yeah, I'll do it. The only reason I'm even there is because of the experience."

Emily and I throw our coffees away, and then she drives us over to Illusion. The club isn't open yet, so we use the employee entrance, and I search for Gregor. After about five minutes, I hear he's in Christian's office, so the two of us head to Christian's office and knock on the door.

"Ladies, can I help you?" Christian asks.

"Yes, actually. Do you mind if we come in?"

Christian nods, and we both enter, taking a seat across from his desk. Gregor shuts the door behind the two of us, so we have some decent privacy.

"What can I help you ladies with?" Christian questions us, his eyes darting between the two of us.

"I'm here to put my two weeks' notice in, but Emily's agreed to take my shifts. She's already picked up some shifts, so we thought that would be better than hiring someone else and having to deal with training them."

Christian blusters a laugh, "I'm sorry to see you go. You're a great employee, Amelia. I appreciate the thought you both put into making sure we wouldn't be short-staffed. Gregor and I were actually speaking a few minutes ago about getting a more permanent schedule for Emily, so I think this works out great."

Great, this is one less thing I have to worry about. Now all I need to do is tell Ruslan I'm carrying his child. If only it didn't make me so damn nervous.

Chapter Twenty-Four

Ruslan

My brothers and sister offered to tail Amelia while she was out with Emily since I've been handling things with Carter. They're only staying here for a few more days, and then they're all heading back to Grozny, but the more I think about it, the more I feel as though I can't leave Atlanta yet. I mean, I know I have to leave, but securing everything with the Steeles is so new. I can't leave without having someone from my family stay behind and ensure the Steele family is happy with our products and business relationship. I'm debating asking Lom if he'll stay here for at least a few months, then he can come back home to Grozny once we have completed a successful probationary period with the Steeles.

Eset texted me a bit ago and said Amelia was leaving Illusion, and it looked like Emily was going to drop her off at the hotel. Sure enough, the elevator door's opening now. I look up from my phone to see Amelia walking down the hallway. She's biting at her bottom lip, and her hands are shaking a tad. It makes me think she's nervous, but I don't know why she'd be so nervous.

"*Malen'kiy krolik*, come. Tell me what's troubling you." Amelia comes over to me and sits next to me on the couch. I place my hand on hers and hold hers firmly, waiting for her to speak.

Amelia takes a few moments before she says anything. She takes in a deep breath and lets it go, then tells me something I never expected to hear her say so soon. "Ruslan, I'm pregnant."

I swallow hard at her admission and watch her features. She's nervously looking around and then tries to look at me for a moment. I think she might be worried about my reaction to this news, and while I didn't expect this, I'm not disappointed in the least bit. Most men my age have already finished having their families, or they're just now getting started.

"How do you feel about it?" I'm not worried about myself. I want to know what Amelia's thoughts are. I want to know if she's comfortable with keeping this pregnancy before I get my hopes up.

"I'm shocked, to say the least, but I think I'm just surprised. I… I didn't expect something like this to happen so soon and because it did, it's kind of thrown me for a loop. You know?"

I chuckle at her answer. I wasn't exactly expecting to get her pregnant so soon, either. "Yes, well, it did happen very fast now, didn't it?"

Amelia nods, and I can see she's still nervous about it. "Yeah."

Amelia doesn't say anything for a few moments, so I tug her against me and wrap an arm around her. I don't know if she realizes it, but she's the most precious thing in the entire world to me. "I'm elated, really. I want to be a father, and I knew I'd be one eventually, but you've given me a precious gift. One I might not be so deserving of yet."

Amelia cranes her neck up to stare at me, and I wait for her to speak. "You are deserving of anything you want, Ruslan. I was terrified you'd be upset about this. I was so scared you'd think I was trying to trap you or something, honestly."

"If we both look at it, I was the one to trap you. Wasn't I?" I laugh, and Amelia shakes her head and smiles. She doesn't like my joke, but it is a bit ironic.

If I really think about it, I never found the right woman to have a child with. I knew one day I'd find someone who was as intelligent as she was nurturing. That woman is Amelia. She has no idea how important she is to me, but I work on showing her every day.

Amelia begins sniffling, and I peer down at her, noticing tears sliding down her cheeks. "Oh, Amelia. Why are you crying? There's no need. Everything is fine."

"I've been so overwhelmed. All day I was convincing myself you'd leave me."

"My sweet Amelia," I run a hand over her face and hold her as close as I can against me. "I'd never leave the mother of my child, especially when I'm undoubtedly in love with her." The moment I make my feelings known, Amelia looks up at me. It's like she thinks she couldn't have possibly heard me correctly, but I'm speaking from the heart.

"I'm in love with you too. I think I've really felt it over the past couple of weeks, but I was afraid to say anything. I'm not a woman who likes being rejected, so that fear can be a dark cloud over my shoulders some days."

"I'd never reject you. Not in the least bit." I kiss the top of her head, and Amelia wraps her arms around me, snuggling her body against mine. This is what I want. This is what I want to do every day for the rest of my life. I want her holding onto me like this. "There is something I wanted to speak to you about while you're here."

Amelia scoots up on the couch a bit and slides her feet under her. "Okay, now you have me nervous."

"My time in Atlanta is coming to an end. My place is in Grozny, and that's where I need to be the face of the Umarova family. I only came here for a few weeks to secure a working relationship with a colleague, but I stayed because of you. I stayed here because I knew this was your home… but I hope our home is now with each other."

Amelia squeezes my hand and smiles lightly. "I thought you might have to leave soon, and I'd hoped you'd extend the invitation to me. When I found out I was pregnant earlier, I put my two weeks' notice in at

Illusion. Emily's actually going to take the rest of my shifts since she wants to get more steady work anyway."

"That's great… and I'm glad you quit."

"I figured you wouldn't want your future baby mama to be walking around in a short skirt at a club."

"Yes, well, it wouldn't exactly be something I hoped for." I laugh, and Amelia laughs too.

It feels as though the chaos in my life is slowly coming to an end. I've dealt with Anzor and found out a lot of secrets along the way. And Carter is no longer a problem for Amelia. The two of us are free from our pasts, and I think we're both ready for this new chapter of our lives. I only hope my father is looking down on me and is proud of the steps I've taken. He'd probably say I took long enough, but I'm sure it would be in jest.

"I know leaving here isn't ideal for you, and I know you will want your cousin to come to visit quite often. I will make sure Emily has plane tickets for whenever she wants to visit, and we will have a bedroom ready for her in our home." I didn't call the house my home. I called it our home because Amelia is a very big part of my life. She's one thing I hope to never lose, and I'll do whatever I need to make sure she and our child are happy.

"Thank you so much." Amelia's moved to tears, and they're streaming down her beautiful face. I wipe them away with my hands, but I'm caught staring at her in awe.

The more I think about it, the more I realize I never want her out of my life. "Marry me." I can't believe I spoke out loud. I was thinking about how much I wanted to marry her, and I blurted it out like an absolute fool. This isn't the way I wanted to ask her at all. I wanted flowers, the ring, the whole nine yards.

"Wait, what?"

"I'm sorry, I didn't plan on ever asking you like this, but I want to marry you. I hope you want to marry me, too. The more I think about it, the more I realize I can't imagine a life without you in it, Amelia. I don't want to live life if you're not here by my side. I want you to be my wife, so will you become Mrs. Umarova?"

"Amelia Umarova does have a nice ring to it."

I smile from ear to ear and pull her into a kiss. "That it does," I mumble against her lips, very well knowing I'm the happiest man on the face of the planet. This woman is my fiancée, and she'll soon be my wife. The only thing I need to do is take her ring shopping and have her pick out the ring of her dreams because as long as I'm beside her, I'll make sure every one of her dreams comes true.

Chapter Twenty-Five

Amelia

I can hardly believe this right now. Ruslan asked me to marry him, and I said yes. I said yes to marrying a man I've only known for a few months. A man who I met under very dark circumstances, where I was unsure if I was even going to make it out alive. Then he surprised me with his actions, and since then, he's continued to do so.

I'm going to be Amelia Umarova very soon, and it really does have a nice ring to it. It sounds beautiful.

"You have made me the happiest man in the world, *malen'kiy krolik*. You're giving me a child and becoming my wife. My life couldn't be any better."

I lean further against Ruslan and press a kiss to his neck. I doubt he realizes it, but when he came into my life, he saved me—quite literally. "I'd have to agree with you." I smile at him and take my lips away from his neck. I place my hands where my lips just were and seal my lips against his. His lips are as soft as ever, and his hands skirt along my body.

He breaks the kiss for a moment and looks into my eyes. "I want us to buy a new place in Grozny, a place that's our home, not just mine."

I narrow my eyes at him. Just because his townhome is his doesn't mean I don't like it. "I love the home you have now. It's absolutely breathtaking."

"It is, but I purchased it as a single man, not as an adult. We have a little one on the way, and all those stairs are a hazard, yes?"

He isn't wrong, but I know he's trying to take a mile with this inch. "We can put up baby gates when the time comes. There are ways our little one will be safe, darling." I try to assure him, but I see on his face that he isn't convinced.

"I think we need a fresh start, and I think we should look for real estate in Grozny now. I want to have a meeting set up by the time we arrive back home." Ruslan's making his opinion known, and I shake my head at it.

"I don't think we need to get another house. The one we have is already so beautiful, not to mention charming."

"Yes, well, I wouldn't sell it. Just in case you'd want to go back to it at some point. Eset and Nazyr will need a place to live now that our mother has cast us all out."

What is he talking about? "I knew you and your mother had a falling out, but why did Eset and Nazyr?"

"They were with me and took part in my actions. My mother technically owns the home they were living in, and I know they're not welcome there. I've already arranged for movers to go and collect their things. The last thing I want is for our mother to go through their personal items and burn or trash them. Especially Eset's paintings. They're beautiful creations that have taken hours upon hours to create." One thing I've noticed about Ruslan is how much he loves his sister's creativity.

"Maybe we could commission your sister to create something beautiful for us," I suggest, and Ruslan smiles brightly.

"Eset would really love that."

"Then we'll have to do it. So, do you want a new place because of the baby and us being together or because your siblings have nowhere to return home to?"

Ruslan sinks back on the couch a bit more. "It's a bit of both, really. I want them to have a safe place to rest their heads, yes, but I also want us to have a fresh start too."

"Okay, then I'm on board for looking at houses. I just didn't want to spend money unless you absolutely needed to. You might have a lot of it, but I don't like to spend for any silly reasons."

"Speaking of money, I want to pay off all your debts from the identity theft, Amelia. We know who did it, and I have the ability to completely replenish your credit and savings. You're to be my wife, and I know the stress of all this has heavily burdened you. I don't want it to do that any longer.

Ruslan pulls out his phone before I can even make a comment about what he's said, and he's pulling up what looks to be a real estate app on his phone.

"Ruslan, are you serious?"

He cocks one brow. "When do I joke about things such as this?"

Never. He never jokes about these sorts of things. I don't bother answering because I know a reply isn't needed or warranted.

"You're really looking at homes right now? We haven't even discussed anything about what we're looking for."

Ruslan eyes me up and down and cackles a bit as he does it. "I know you like the back of my hand, Amelia. You enjoy being in the center of the city, so you'll be able to go on a stroll in the park or stop at a local coffee shop. There are small food stands all around the parks, and the weather is always gorgeous. You wouldn't want to be in the suburbs because it would be more driving for you and Danill. You'd appreciate something a bit easier, nestled in the heart of Grozny. I'll make sure we're in a building that accepts children, and I'm sure you'll make friends once we move."

The more Ruslan speaks, the more it becomes evident he does know me like the back of his hand. He scrolls on his phone and lands on one building specifically. He taps on it and looks at the floor plan first. I'm peering over his shoulder at his phone, and it's a four-bedroom, three-bath condo with two balconies. One of them is to the side, and the other is on the back. The balcony on the back has a small pool.

After reviewing the floor plan, we went over the photos the listing agent took. The kitchen is big and is pretty much all white. There are a bunch of black squares in the tile on the floor, which gives it a decent contrast, and the black color carries throughout the kitchen in subtle ways. It seems so modern and beautiful, and it would be a dream to cook in a kitchen like that.

The living area is massive and has gold wallpaper lining the walls. It's the type of wallpaper that you know had to have cost quite a bit of money. There's a matching gold carpet on the floor with cream-colored designs on it, and a bit of black is in it as well.

Next to the living room is a small sitting room, and that's where the door that leads into the condo is. It's a bit bigger than a foyer, big enough to have two couches lining the walls. There are coat hangers and some sort of dresser with candles and small décor as well.

We look over the bedrooms, and each is just as big as the others. One of them is even plain in a gray color and would be perfect to start a nursery.

Overall, this place looks amazing. "What do you think of it?"

"I think it's gorgeous." I waste no time telling Ruslan exactly how I feel.

He nods once. "All right, then I'll schedule an appointment for us in three days."

"Three days?"

"Yes, we'll leave for Grozny the day after tomorrow. It'll give us one day to rest. The more I think about it, the more I don't want you doing too much right now. I'm sure you'll get tired a lot easier, and I want you to rest as much as you can."

Ruslan cares so much about our child and me already. He seemed so eager to look at listings the day we arrived in Grozny, and now he's willing to wait a day. He's putting my needs and our child's above his own excitement, and I'm sure it's a sneak peek at what kind of father he'll be.

I take Ruslan's phone out of his hand and sit it down on the coffee table, then straddle his hips on the couch. I'm wearing a purple dress that fans out around my hips. He raises both of his brows as I make my movement, staring me up and down. He knows what I'm doing, and he can't fool me one bit.

I cup his face with both of my hands, and he smirks. "You're a very determined woman."

"Yes, I know. And you're very willing to give me what I want," I point out with a sly smile, and Ruslan throws his head back in laughter. It's the deep-belly type of laughter I love to hear from him.

"You're right, *malen'kiy Krolik*. You're very right." Ruslan comments as I grind my hips against his. I want his cock to come to life because I need him. I need to feel his hands all over my body. I need to feel all the pleasure I know he'll bring. Earlier today, I was so stressed out, and now I need him to take it away from me.

He grabs my hand and puts it over his hardening shaft, so I run my hand along it until he's rock-hard. I lick my lips and swallow because I know he's going to fuck me well. I can see it in his eyes, how he's trying so desperately to hold back even though he doesn't want to.

Ruslan paws at the buttons of my dress and pops every one of them free. He pulls the cups of my bra down and wraps his lips around one nipple, sucking and gnawing while he rolls the other between his fingers. I moan lightly at his actions, and my pussy ignites with more need than I know what to do with.

I roll my hips against his, and he takes his hands down to his pants to undo them. He pulls his cock out and moves between my thighs, shoving my panties to the side as he sinks me down onto his hardness. I release a breath when he's completely inside me, and Ruslan places his hands on my hips.

I rock up and down on him, but he quickly moves my body to the speed he wants. It isn't long before he's lifting me off his cock and putting me on my back on the couch. He rids himself of his pants and boxers and pushes my legs back. They settle right over his shoulders, and he rams himself deep inside me. I'm so wet that every time he drills inside of me, a sloshing sound can be heard. He wastes no time bringing me to the cusp of my orgasm, and he soon follows me, but he drags it out as long as he can.

This is why I love Ruslan Umarova because he's only ever made me feel cherished and appreciated. There isn't any other man on this planet who can make me feel this great, and he's the one I'll be spending the rest of my life with.

Ruslan is everything I need… and nothing I knew I craved.

Epilogue

Ruslan

One Year Later

As I sit on the couch looking over emails from this morning, Karim's low cry pulls me from my work. Amelia was up with him most of the night, so I didn't wake her up this morning. I didn't want to. She's been exhausted a majority of the time since Karim's birth, and I told her she needs to take care of herself too. She tells me it's her job to take care of Karim and that I need to focus on my work, but Karim isn't just her child. He's mine, too, and therefore, it's my responsibility to step up. I'll never be the type of father who says he's "babysitting" or "watching" his own kids. They're going to be my children, and I want to split the duties between Amelia and me. After all, she can't be running on empty all the time.

I rise and head for his nursery, which Amelia decorated herself. I may have put together the furniture in here and hung the shelves on the walls, but she had the entire concept. It's an African safari theme, and she has everything from an oversized stuffed giraffe in the corner of the room to a hamper that looks like an elephant. She even had Eset paint a lion, and it hangs over Karim's crib. It's something that doesn't look too childish, and I think as Karim grows up, it could always stay here in his room.

I scoop him into my arms and hush him, but he doesn't calm

down. I check his diaper, and sure enough, it's soiled. I whisper to him as I put him on the changing table and proceed to clean him up, finally putting a new diaper on him. I take it upon myself to change his clothes while I'm at it. He might be a bit cold, so I put him in a onesie. He really likes these because they cover his feet.

Once he's freshly changed, Karim calms down, and it's obvious he's awake for a while. I carry him in one arm to the kitchen and pull out some breast milk from the fridge. Amelia pumps, and it goes into this bag. Each time she pumps, it goes into a different one, and we keep fresh milk in the fridge for when she's out of the house or asleep. I never want to wake her unless I have to. I pour the milk into a bottle and insert it into the bottle warmer. In a couple of minutes, he'll have a bottle warmed perfectly. It'll be warm enough to keep him happy but not too hot to burn his lips.

Lom's supposed to be arriving here any minute, but he told me that right as Karim started crying. He's in town for a couple of days, and then he's returning to Atlanta to handle something. He's been there making sure everything's going well with the Steeles, and it's been flowing perfectly. There hasn't been one hiccup with them, and I'm grateful for it. In the beginning, there were a lot of people happy that I took what belonged to me, but as time settled, a few issues arose. Issues my brothers and I had handled before they ever came to the light of day.

Lom has a key to the condo Amelia and I purchased. It's the one we looked at that day in Atlanta. We came here and fell in love with not only the condo but also the location. The balcony was a big plus for Amelia. She sits outside a lot with Karim. She says she likes the fresh air, but I know she also likes hearing the hustle and bustle of the city.

Nazyr and Eset share the townhome I already owned since our mother did kick them out. I had movers grab whatever she hadn't already destroyed. Nazyr was lucky, but Eset had her entire art studio destroyed by our mother. She had pieces that took days and days to create, but our mother was so furious she ruined whatever she wanted without any regard for my sister's feelings. We all know she thinks she's in the right. She still does. She thinks we were wrong for doing what we did to Anzor, but he deserved it.

After we displayed my stepfather's head in the middle of Grozny, everyone lost it. Some people cheered, thinking his death happened far too late. While some people like my mother tried to publicly condemn his "brutal and unwarranted" murder. It was a joke, really. How people could still try to defend him after everything I know is beyond me.

Footsteps come up behind me, and I turn around, expecting it to be Danill or Nal. Sure enough, it's Lom, but he isn't alone. In tow behind him is Emily, Amelia's cousin. Someone I didn't know was coming today. I knew she'd be here next week, so I cock a brow and look between Lom and Emily.

"Don't tell Amelia. I want this to be a surprise," Emily tells me as she comes over and scoops my son out of my arms. The bottle warmer dings, and she fetches the bottle like she knows exactly what she's doing as she proceeds to feed Karim. "Gosh, you've gotten so big in these short few weeks, little one," she tells him, and I notice Lom staring intently at Emily holding a baby.

It makes me curious if Emily could be the one to tame my wild brother's soul. "Are you all right with Karim?" I ask Emily, and she almost looks annoyed at my question.

"Obviously, go do whatever you two need to do." She waves us off and walks into the living room with Karim. Meanwhile, I take Lom into my office. We didn't even see this on the blueprint of the place when we were looking at it online because it's a safe room. It was a big plus for me, given what I do for a living.

Lom and I both take a seat once we're inside, and I lean back against the leather couch. "How are things in Atlanta?"

"They're going great. I actually wanted to speak to you about coming back home. Atlanta's nice, but I'm growing bored of the view," Lom comments, and I notice he swallows hard.

"Bored of the view or bored of Emily?" I ask him out of the blue. I'd rather cut straight to the chase, and I await Lom to comment. I thought he'd immediately be firing back, but he hasn't.

"Emily is of no concern to you," Lom hisses, glaring at me with all his might. "I want to come back to Grozny because it's where I belong. Our business with the Steele family has gone on without a hitch, and it's time for me to come back, brother. It's been longer than we needed, actually."

I smirk at my brother's attitude, and it confirms everything I thought. He cares for Emily. Though, I wonder if he's admitted it to himself yet. I can't wait to see how this plays out between them. I want my brother to find happiness just as I have because there's nothing else in the world like it—especially since my wedding to Amelia is taking place next week.

My life couldn't get any better.

Your Free Gifts

Wow we hope we've satisfied your romance itch... for now. If you've enjoyed reading about these alpha males, please take a minute to leave a review.

Are you craving for more dark mafia romance stories? Don't forget to claim your FREE exclusive access to the prequel by joining our VIP newsletter.

You'll also be the first to hear about upcoming new releases, giveaways, future discounts, and much more.

Click here to sign up and get your FREE access to The Umarova Crime Family Prequel now! https://BookHip.com/MXSLKNV

See you on the inside,
Ivy Black and Elizabeth Knox

Printed in Great Britain
by Amazon